BYRD RANCH LEGACY

Byrd Ranch Series - Book 3

JANA DAHMEN

Publishing Coordinator – Sharon Kizziah-Holmes
Cover Art – Jana Dahmen

Paperback-Press
an imprint of A & S Publishing
A & S Holmes, Inc.

ISBN -13: 978-1-960499-84-4

ACKNOWLEDGMENTS

My friend and husband, Marv Dahmen, has been a bachelor in his own home while I have spent the whole month of January 2024 finishing the Byrd Ranch Legacy. He has given me all the love, support, and space I have needed. It helps Marv is an artist and musician. He understands being obsessed beyond reason with a creative project! The two of us have always made a good team. I love him to the moon and back!

Sharon Kizziah-Holmes has been an inspiration to me since the day we met. Not only is she my publishing coordinator with Paperback Press, but I'm proud to call her my friend.

The Women's Getaway and Writing Retreat I attend twice a year has been instrumental in getting me back into writing. I'd like to thank Terry McDermid for hosting and to thank all of the authors who attend and help me when I need encouragement.

PROLOGUE

I lay hidden, observing the camp. I had no interest in the whole gang. There was only one man I was after.

Making me jump, the first rifle shot cracked the calm just before dawn. It was clear as a lightning strike and almost deafening. It came from the direction of JD's position on the rim above the den of thieves.

The band of outlaws was instantly put on alert, and the men were sent scurrying around like a colony of red ants. The posse had found the camp, and a rain of bullets would soon shower down on the outlaws' heads.

Caught with their britches down, the survival instinct took over. It was every man for himself. Men with sleep crusted in their eyes panicked in confusion. Some clad only in long johns, scurried out of makeshift shelters with gun belts slung low on the hips of their drawers. They carried boots and rifles.

Like harvest ants from an ant hill, they poured out headed in different directions. Nervous horses broke through a rope corral and ran a farther piece down the canyon. Each bandit was out to defend himself. Clay had made a preliminary count yesterday, and I saw the eight men and two women. The women fled for cover into the bushes.

The coward's guns started blazing in complete chaos. The outlaws were disorganized and shooting blindly, wasting their bullets. I knew where Stone and Clay were positioned, but neither had fired a shot yet. The boys were waiting for their pa or the marshal to shoot again.

They didn't have long to wait. The reports of two rifles fractured the air coming from the direction of the two lawmen. It was the incentive the boys had been waiting to hear. They joined in, and one of them picked off a man from his vantage point on the opposite side.

In the melee I saw a man slip under the back side of a tent and take off running. He jumped on the first horse he reached. He was getting away, and there was no doubt in my mind who the rat bastard was! It was the captain abandoning his ship. Alex Johns was leaving his men to sink or swim!

This couldn't have worked out more perfectly for me. I'd hoped to get the chance to confront this thug alone. Filly and I flew in hot pursuit. Only Clay and Stone knew I was lurking somewhere around.

Filly ran like a good girl, and soon I'd gotten close enough to fire a shot on the run. I shot my handgun and hit Alex Johns in his shoulder. It entered exactly where I'd aimed. I wanted him looking at me in the face when I killed him.

The force of the bullet knocked him off the horse, and his gun flew to the side somewhere out of his reach as he fell face forward on the ground. The frantic animal set sail for Kansas without ever slowing down!

I praised Filly for her performance and rubbed her neck before I dismounted. By this time, Alex had managed to turnover, but he was disarmed. He'd drawn a knife though, but I easily kicked it out of his hand. I stood over him looking down and pointing my gun at his blackened heart.

He must have been surprised to see a woman had taken him down. I laughed at him like a maniac! He was older and so was I. He had an old scar on his cheek now, but I recognized him alright.

"Who are you?" he sputtered.

CHAPTER 1

SARI'S CREW

~ *Sari 1892*

An impatient, disgusted, Sari cupped hands to her mouth and hollered, "Stone, Clay! Hey! Stone, Clay, you buzzards! Can you hear me? Stone? Clay?" Her feathers were all kinds of ruffled. This was so typical of her younger brothers to run off and leave her behind.

How dare those damn, dumb inconsiderate brothers to run off and leave me again!

The constant hot wind was coming from the south, blowing directly into her face as she struggled to holler above the howl as loudly as she could. The power of the ragged gusts was pesky. The dry, red sand lifted into the air burning her eyes and making her teeth feel gritty. This was one of those days with gusts so intense the force blew the spit right out of Sari's mouth.

She was a sight with her straw hat tied on her head with

a faded bandana! This was not unusual in West Texas. Turning her horse to the east, she hollered again and again. She repeated the call to the west with still no answer being heard over the wailing gale.

She might punch Stone once she found him. He'd never punch her back though. She liked to think she was older than him, but no one actually knew the date of his birth. Still a baby, he came to live with Ma and Pa after she was born. Then Clay was for sure born several months after Sari right here on Byrd Ranch.

The family Bible had the whole list of family names and when each one of us was born. The big Bible went as far back as our great-great grandparents even before there was a Byrd Ranch. Stone's written birthdate was the same day Ma had found him on the prairie. So, in writing, at least, she was recorded as the older.

Cousin Maisy was older than Sari, but she first came here when Uncle Cole married her mother, Qynne. They had fallen in love at first sight. He'd built his own house by what he named Qynne's Canyon before he went to get Maisy and her ma.

Qynne's Canyon was one of the most picturesque places on the ranch. Sari spent a lot of time there with Maisy. They were more like sisters than cousins. Now Maisy had a little brother, Rhett. There was a whole flock of little Byrds running around the ranch, but Sari, Stone, Clay, and Maisy were tied together by the closeness of their ages. Ma said a special cord bound them together in the tapestry of life since they were the first children here besides pa and the uncles, of course.

If one was in trouble, then the other three usually were too. Many times, the four had tearfully endured their punishments together. Sari certainly didn't care to ponder on the time they had been caught passing around the pint of whiskey. Nobody could sit for the next two days.

She kicked Clover, her dapple-gray mare, into a full

gallop running east. After three-quarters of a mile, Clover slowed and started climbing the familiar upward grade to reach the top of Frank's Hill.

Closer to the crest, cedars grew fuller and taller. They sheltered the plateau from the worrisome winds. The heat of the day distributed the sweet, pungent fragrance of the sticky cedar sap. Sari inhaled the familiar smell laced in the breeze.

Frank's lone grave rested in solitude under an umbrella of beautiful evergreen growth. The thick, white marble tombstone was engraved with the name Frank McGill. The whole family reverently tended his grave in the spring and fall every year. Whoever he once was when he lived and breathed, he was buried with honor right here on Byrd Ranch.

This man had lain covered in this spot since 1877. Sari had come with Ma to this place even when she was too young to realize a man died and was buried here. As she'd gotten older and more independent, she and her crew of cohorts in mischief had continued to gravitate to the top of the quiet hill. This isolated and peaceful spot had become their favorite hideout away from the eyes of adults.

They raced their first ponies to Frank's Hill, thinking it was an adventurous trek and much farther away from ranch headquarters than just short of a mile. After Maisy came here to live, she rode with Sari on Stranger, her big, mild-mannered gelding. The four oldest cousins became thick as thieves and used this hill as their not-so-secret or innocent hideout.

Well, sure enough, Clover, we found the pesky boys and Maisy up here loafing in the clouds!

Maisy, the traitor, was picking wildflowers off in the distance. No doubt, the assorted blossoms she held in her hand were destined to fill the piece of cracked Indian pottery sitting at the base of Frank's tombstone.

All the kids really knew about this man was his name,

but Frank McGill held special places in the hearts of the Byrd family. The grave of this mysterious person drew the children like bees to nectar. This was the perfect setting for the young rebels to share secrets, swap dreams, conjure up exciting stories, and to plan their shenanigans.

Before Sari dismounted Clover, she cupped her hands around her mouth and yelled in Maisy's direction, "Well! I might have known I'd find you up here with 'em, Maisy Byrd! Where were you when I was stuck pulling weeds in the garden this morning? Don't pretend you forgot! We all eat those vegetables, ya know! Maybe loafers won't get a share this year."

Clay, lying on the short stone wall Grey had built as a border around the grave, agreed with Sari's idea in a backhanded way.

"Good thinkin', Sari! I could do with fewer green beans on my plate."

"Shut up, Clay! I'll wrestle you off the wall and down the hill, I swear, I will! I just finished sweating through the bean rows of which you speak. Thank you for the idea! I'm gonna make sure you get extra string beans on your plate from now to Christmas!

"How come ya'll boys didn't help or at least wait for me to get loose from Ma, so I could ride up here with you? Why is it fair I had to help Ma in the table garden, and ya'll didn't? I can't wait to hear your excuse, Maisy."

Maisy was close enough now to answer without straining her voice.

"I don't know about the boys, but I was cleaning the horse barn."

From the look on her face, Sari wasn't ready to wind her tirade down anytime soon.

Maisy added, "I can stand mucking stalls any day of the week but pulling stupid weeds, uh, not so much, Sari!"

Drawing out Sari's name, Stone offered his two cents worth from where he lay.

"Clay and I were out before daybreak mending fences with Pa. The breeze is cooler before the sun has a chance to heat it. Broken fences make for hard work, Sari, and by the time we got back, our tails were draggin' in the dirt. Try gettin' up earlier to do yer chores, why don't cha? It's much cooler then.

"Besides Girl, seems to me, you've an awful short memory. Don't you recollect Clay and me plowing the same garden you were weedin' so you could plant those beans? The two old onery plow mules were a tiresome trial as I recall. It was in the cold March wind too if I'm rememberin' it right. We dang nearly froze the tips of our noses off in the cold, bitter wind.

"Clay and I did exactly what Pa told us to do like always. Anyway, Sari, you can't call today runnin' away when you knew all along exactly where to find us. Keeping old Frank company is an important job. Somebody's gotta take time out to do it even if there's work to be done."

While Stone was giving Sari an unappreciated lecture, he hadn't bothered to sit up from where he was stretched out on the soft, cool grass. He hadn't even bothered to remove the battered, old, sweat-stained Stetson covering his face from the light.

Sari remembered when he'd found the worn-out hat thrown-away on the ranch's trash pile behind the bunkhouse. He'd rescued it before the pile went up in flames. Sari's opinion was it should have been left to burn even though Stone swore it had character and his kind of personality.

Stone was a big, strong, curly, red-headed fellow with a ruddy complexion, copper freckles, and an agreeable disposition. He was two heads taller than Sari, but he never used his size to win an argument with her to claim he was older.

The boys' brotherly love for Sari was solid, and they took her haranguing in stride. Sari complained their protectiveness was tiring and cumbersome, but the brothers watched out for her, almost always. Maybe this was why she insisted on trying everything her brothers tried. She rarely could be deterred once she took a notion to do something.

CHAPTER 2

POOR JUDGEMENT TIMES FOUR

Clay was sitting up now on the sandstone wall of Frank's memorial yard. He was practicing the fine art of rolling a flawless cigarette. Learning to roll a bona fide cig was not as easy as the ranch hands made it look.

He'd been watching them of late, and they made it appear to be an attainable skill to master. So far, Clay's fingers worked together more like ten thumbs, but he wouldn't give up trying until he was satisfied with the product.

He'd just laid a line of tobacco on the thin, tissue paper rectangle resting on his thigh. A small bleached domestic pouch of tobacco was hanging off a yellow string dangling from his teeth. He carefully fisted the bag and pulled it closed with one hand without unsettling the precarious paper or the fixings he balanced. He spit the string aside leaving his hands free to even out the tiny pieces of chopped tobacco leaves. Next, he curled the flimsy paper around the baccy.

The resulting cylinder was bumpy and bulged more on one end than the other. The thin white tissue paper was wrinkled but it would do. He lifted the untidy roll carefully to his lips, flicking out his tongue to moisten the narrow adhesive strip on one edge of the paper to seal it together securely. When he held it up for inspection, he sighed. He wouldn't call it good, but at least it was an improvement over the last one.

Sari had been watching him the whole time with a smirk cocked to one side of her face.

"Ma will skin you alive if she catches you! Anyway, I'm better at rolling a smoke than you are. I'll roll the next one."

"No, go roll one for yourself, Sari. I'm doin' just fine, thanks. I don't need any help."

"Nah, I can roll 'em, but I don't like to smoke 'em. I can't stand the nasty taste of the smoke in my mouth. Besides, smoking isn't lady-like. I just wanted to prove to you I can roll one better."

Both boys belly laughed louder and longer than necessary. Stone laughed so hard he found it necessary to sit up and position his trashed hat to the top of his head. Once he got himself under control, he pointed out, "Sari, half the things you do aren't lady-like. I'm afraid you've been riding tomboy-wild too long."

Clay walked over to the gravestone and put the unlit cig at the base of the marble stone where the broken pottery sat. It now held Maisy's offering of wildflowers. The children made it a habit to leave small offerings for Frank McGill. Their parents, Grey and Mary Ann Byrd, had never told them who this man was, but they'd surely taught their children to respect him without question.

Nobody seemed to know who he'd been when he was alive or how he ended up here on Byrd Ranch dead. The aunts and uncles were tight-lipped whenever his name was mentioned. The family secret wasn't a topic open for discussion around the dinner table or anywhere else. It was just understood Frank McGill lived and died, nothing more.

His grave was a happy place and well-visited though. The four found it fascinating to come here among the flowers and cedars. It was a favorite destination for the cousins to ride their horses, eat picnics, and just hang out together. The secrecy didn't keep them from sharing speculations about Frank's identity. Some of the stories were quite far-fetched.

The intertwined families and hands lived and worked together on Byrd Ranch in homes, bunk houses, and small buildings built by themselves or someone who rested in the family cemetery. Sari's real mother, Elizabeth, was buried there, and her ma, Mary Ann, kept her grave well-tended. Ma never knew her, but she encouraged Aunt Belle to talk about Beth to Sari. Ma didn't want her forgotten.

The official family tree was a crude work of art drawn on an old, tanned hide of a baby buffalo. It hung on a wall in the ranch house office. There was no reference there for Frank McGee, and the name Wisteria, the evil cousin, had been marked out. She poisoned Sari's birth mother over fourteen years ago and had tried twice to kill Sari.

Grey Byrd and Mary Ann Barton married immediately after Beth's death because the tiny Sari wouldn't have survived without a mother. Then Stone came and shortly after, Clay was born. Sari never remembered life without her brothers, Stone and Clay.

Their much younger siblings Ada and Ben were very much loved by them but were tied into the family's history at different times with different strings. They would never quite have the same bond with their three oldest siblings as Sari, Stone, and Clay shared.

Stone said totally out of the blue to no one in particular, "You know, I've been hankering to ride a long-horned steer. Ya'll 'member the old man who rode one down the middle of the street on the Fourth of July? They were both decked out in red, white, and blue ribbons. I've been thinking a lot about how the crowd admired them lately.

"There's that old longhorn, Tex, in the pasture not far from here. He wears a braided bridle and lets us pet 'im but otherwise he serves no real purpose. He's just an old pet and not good for anything but burnin' hay. Wouldn't it be somethin' to ride him down main street?

"I've been considering givin' it a try! Any takers want to go and watch me break him in?"

Well, what seemed like a great idea in theory to the crew was not even remotely an acceptable idea to an old, retired lead steer! Sure, he'd gladly take a treat now and then, but it was as chummy as he cared to get.

The cow punchers, years ago, on the Byrd Ranch trail drives used to give him a biscuit or two as he sauntered through camp begging after supper. He had taken the handouts because it was his idea. Tex would never have stood for a cowpoke to climb on his back and kick him with spurs. The dominant steer would have ditched the foolish cow puncher, torn up the camp, and may even have taken the chuckwagon apart. No, likely Tex had no predisposition whatsoever to put up with mischief from this crazy, four-kid crew.

In his prime the longhorn proudly wore a bell around his neck and led herds through miles and miles on the demanding rigors of several trail drives. He may have been put out to pasture at the end of the era, but retirement had done nothing to cool his superior inbred attitude. He was still every bit a hard-headed lead steer.

Before this fateful afternoon was over, Old Tex would be the last one left standing. Sari, Stone, Clay, and Maisy would tuck their broken tails between their legs in humiliation and be in no hurry to show themselves at home.

The sorry bunch would ride into ranch headquarters with their heads hanging low, and there'd be hell to pay when Grey and Cole got a good look at their oldest children. The whole lot would learn a lesson they'd never forget.

Do not underestimate an elderly, lead longhorn named Tex who'd retired to the pasture and only wanted to eat and be left alone!

CHAPTER 3

TEX, THE LEAD LONGHORN

Lead steers were valuable during the days of the big trail drives. Only a few steers were born with an over-active, bossy, leadership mentality. No mortal man could teach them be such leaders. A herd of average beef cattle would settle methodically into the rhythm of a long drive if given one arrogant lead steer, flanked by point riders, to mindlessly follow.

A natural like Tex couldn't stand the thought of cattle getting ahead of him. He was their leader and always determined to be ahead of the others. The most famous lead steer of all time was Old Blue. He belonged to Charles Goodnight of the JA Ranch. On Goodnight's first cattle drive, Old Blue passed all the other steers until he made it to the front. The herd grew accustomed to following him and yielded to his self-appointed rank.

No cow puncher ever had to round up Goodnight's Old Blue and drive him to the front of the procession each morning. No Siree! When the men set the herd into motion,

Old Blue came right up and took his rightful place.

At the end of the day, the drivers wrapped his clapper in cloth, so the herd couldn't hear his bell ringing and think it was time to move out. He also walked around the cowboys' camp in the evenings looking for handouts. The pushers were more than happy to reward his valuable help.

Old Blue was a strikingly tall mulberry-colored steer with horns spread especially wide. From tip to tip the span was approximately forty-five inches. His true color was actually gunmetal-blue, but the cowboys called it mulberry.

Old Blue commanded the point position on more than eight drives from the Palo Duro Canyon, where Goodnight's famous JA Ranch was located, to Dodge City, Kansas where beef cattle earned ranchers the best prices per head.

The crew had never heard any of this history. They didn't fathom there was danger in Stone's foolhardy notion. Since he'd been forced into retirement, Tex had grown comfortable, lazy, and content being left alone. At his core he still had the ornery disposition of the head steer. Stone, Clay, Sari, and Maisy failed to realize Tex might not be the old docile pet they'd pegged him.

The old boy was conditioned to approach, stand still for pets and sweet words, and to wait for treats. It was deceiving behavior since his takeover attitude was very much intact and lying dormant behind his big brown, placid eyes. Right between his ears, programed in his brain, a lead, bell steer was hiding.

As expected, he ran up to the fence once he heard the voices of the four kids calling. He was anticipating a tasty snack but when none was offered, he grew wary and anxious. The youngsters failed to notice his slightly pawing feet as their excitement built. This was a frolic to them.

They climbed through the gaps in the wires instead of staying out of Tex's enclosure. After the kindness of a few rubs, the two boys lured him to a cedar fence post and tied him with a rope. Makeshift reins were wrapped around his neck. Tex made a breathy, nervous snort of air and became restless.

With no warning, Stone leaped onto his back. Tex didn't sign up for this! He made three bucks with front feet in the air and then the back feet in the air. The last buck launched the heavy boy into the sky.

Dazed, Stone landed on his back a few feet away looking up at the clear turquoise-blue heavens. Immediate pain seared through his left arm, exploding in his shoulder. Clay quickly helped him get a safer distance away from the steer's hooves. Stone cradled his arm and shook his head a few times moaning and cursing before he spoke.

"Dang, Tex caught me off guard! I don't know what happened to spook him."

Bloody abrasions were on Stone's face, and the injured shoulder was a source of great pain. He supported the elbow with his other hand.

Clay said too loudly, "I think you're just too heavy for him, Brother. He's old. Let's see how I get along with him."

First, Clay talked into his ear and scratched behind it. Clay thought Tex had settled down but apparently his calm demeanor meant he was just waiting for the next hand to be dealt. He didn't mean to be ridden by any amount of weight. When Clay mounted, he wasn't even seated well before the boy flew through the air. The wind was completely knocked out of his sails when he smacked chest first on the hard ground.

He couldn't breathe for a long while. The other three were afraid he was dead until he finally drew in a long, roaring intake of air followed by wheezing and coughing. Clay struggled to sit up, clutching his chest which was on fire from the impact. The pristine brim of the black hat he coveted was bent all to heck, and the hat itself was covered from the clouds of dust boiled around him.

Maisy and Stone were both assessing Clay's injuries when they heard a coyote-like yell from the direction of Tex. Sari yelled, "My turn!".

"No, Sari! You'll get hurt! Get back!" Stone called out to no avail because by then it was too late to stop his sister.

"You mean hurt like you and Clay, don't cha? I can ride this old steer!"

"Yeah, you go, Cowgirl," egged on Maisy while staring the boys down. "Show 'em how it's done!" The girls always stuck together and wore britches around the ranch like Maisy's ma. Their aunt Qynne worked and rode hard as a man in the comfortable attire.

Before Clay could give a hoarse warning, Sari took a running start and sprang onto Tex's boney back startling the steer. She only felt his knobby backbone between her legs for a few seconds before he flung her off like an old, limber ragdoll. She landed a few feet away face first.

"Damn! Ouch!" she hollered and cried big tears with a load of dirt turning to mud in her mouth. Not lucky at all, she had landed in a patch of viciously barbed goat head thorns. The vicious stickers penetrated the skin on her face including her tender lip. The long, poisonous barbs even pierced the cloth of her shirt and embedded into her skin like projectiles.

Using his one good arm, Stone helped her crawl to a more hospitable place and started picking the goat heads out of her flesh with one hand, but some were too painful to touch as the toxic substance in the wood was causing swelling around them. Her face and hands were bloody, bruising, and puffy already. Sari tried hard not to scream each time he pulled one of the barbed grass burrs out, but she mostly failed.

Clay was still taking labored breaths when they heard a

commotion. Maisy, the dare devil, had managed to straddle the steer. Things looked good for a few moments, and she actually stayed on longer than the others. Then the steer let out two shrill sounds vibrating from his throat and flapping his nostrils like butterfly wings.

He shook his head, and in a powerful surge he butted the mesquite fencepost where he'd been tied, hard. The post snapped off above the ground. He took off in a dead run with the post and broken wires dragging behind him. When Maisy finally slid off, she landed on top of the barbed wire. Tex never slowed and dragged the girl along with the sharp barbs until he broke loose and ran out of sight.

Maisy screamed over and over like a big mama cat. Stone and Clay were speechless at the ruins around her. Maisy's jeans were in shreds, and the cuts on her legs oozed blood. An ugly goose egg was rising on their cousin's forehead. She was out of it and had even passed out for a couple of minutes at one point.

Stunned and ashamed by their recklessness, no one had anything to say. The devastation had happened so quickly. They were all in shock.

Finally, Stone took his belt off with one hand and used it with Clay's help to loop around his neck and buckle it to make a sling for his arm. It relieved some of the stress on his shoulder. Using his good hand, Stone helped Clay wrap bandanas tightly around Maisy's deepest cuts. The colorful bandages stanched some of the bleeding.

Clay mounted his horse and moved closer to Maisy who was still down. Stone helped Sari with his uninjured arm to lift Maisy up as Clay reached down to pull from the top. It was awkward and Maisy cried through the pain, but she finally sat in front of Clay whimpering and exhausted.

Sari led Stranger behind Clover. She had a red, swollen nose and was smarting from the goat heads. Some had broken off below the skin and burned like being at the door of hell. Tears rolled down her cheeks, but Sari never complained or blamed Stone even once.

Poor Maisy had suffered the worst trauma of them all and sitting on the horse leaning against Clay was tough. The crew took it slowly but steadily riding toward the ranch house. A couple of hands spotted them and galloped to help. They escorted the hurt kids to the kitchen door.

Ma and Aunt Belle took one look at the bedraggled crew and went white as sheets. The men helped them off the horses and carried the girls into the kitchen. One of the cowhands led the horses to the barn. The other rode immediately to Cap Rock to fetch Doc. Belle rang the emergency signal from the back porch alerting Cole, Qynne, Smith, and Grey to hurry home.

Belle had been baking bread pudding for supper, had beef roasting in the oven, and a pot of brown beans was simmering on the stove when the savory kitchen suddenly transformed into an infirmary.

Maisy lay on the table asking for her mama. Mary Ann's three sat in a line on kitchen chairs. Belle put on willow bark tea to brew to help with the pain. The women washed away dirt and blood. They offered soothing comfort, but there was little else they could do but wait on the doctor.

Qynne, Cole, Smith, and Grey arrived about the same time as Doc. There were grim faces all around. Everyone talked in whispers. Belle had water heated for Doc to use. She had a big pot of coffee ready.

Doc tended to Maisy first. She calmed down once Qynne got to her and after a dose of laudanum. Doc let it take effect before he started scrubbing the cuts with soap and water and dousing them with alcohol. The stitches came next. A cold compress made with chipped ice from the cellar icehouse was applied to the lump on her forehead.

Doc dosed Sari with laudanum and removed the remaining thorns. He scrubbed every puncture wound clean and dowsed them with alcohol. Both girls were already feverish.

Stone had a dislocated shoulder. He roared when Doc popped it back into place, but the acute pain relief was immediate. Doc fashioned a cloth sling to take the pressure off of the terribly sore shoulder. He would need to wear it for two days at least.

Clay had recovered from having the wind knocked out of him, but he was stiff, bruised, and sore. Doc checked him over and listened to his lungs. There was a danger of pneumonia in injuries like this, but Doc was satisfied he would be all right.

CHAPTER 4

———◆ ◈ ◆———

A HARD CONVERSATION

Cole and Gray sat in the parlor listening to Sari and Maisy crying. Even Stone, as tough as leather, hollered when Doc manipulated his shoulder back into its socket. Grey combed his fingers through his hair leaving it in disarray. Seeing and hearing their children hurting had been hard on the two papas. The men would have rather been the ones in pain.

Smith had gone with three hands to find Tex and repair the break in the fence. There was a chance the Longhorn had been injured in this fiasco.

Grey and Mary Ann put Sari to bed while Cole helped Qynne, Maisy, and their baby boy, Rhett get settled into a buggy. Belle packed a supper basket for them to take home. Qynne flicked the reins and turned toward Qynne's Canyon to get Maisy tucked into bed. Palo and Stranger were staying at the ranch's horse barn for the night.

Cole joined Grey in the office after his family was on

their way home. Grey broke out the bourbon to dull the knowledge of the ordeal. They were both thankful because the damage could have been a whole lot worse.

Mary Ann walked into the room and raised her eyebrows at the sight of the bottle usually shut up in the bottom desk drawer. She placed Clay's broken hat he cherished off to one side of the office desk. Without smiling, she said Stone and Clay would be joining them directly. Grey studied the broken brim of the hat Clay treated so carefully and shuttered at the thought it could just as easily have been Clay's head broken.

Involuntarily, Grey gritted his teeth making his jaw muscles visibly contract and release rhythmically. What the four oldest Byrd children had done today demonstrated a serious lapse in good judgement. He stared at his two young men as they entered the room bruised and bandaged with their heads contritely down and took the hot seats in front of the desk.

He figured it was only right to let Cole have the first chance to speak since his Maisy had been injured the most severely in the afternoon's debacle.

"Boys," Clay said loudly and sternly, "Your cousin, Maisy and your sister, Sari, got hurt badly today. They both could have been crippled or even killed as well as you two could have suffered the same fates. I always figured Grey and I could count on you to take care of our girls when we weren't there to protect them.

"I am so disappointed you let your pa and me down today. Maisy and Sari will no doubt carry scars from what happened. Every time you notice one, you remember exactly how it got there. You put the girls in harm's way.

"Byrd men always put the welfare of their women first and keep them safe."

Stone spoke up to take the blame.

"Sorry Uncle Cole, Pa, we, uh, this is all my fault. I'm to blame. It was never Clay's idea from the beginning. I'm broken-hearted this happened. The last thing I'd ever do is get the girls hurt."

"I don't care how sorry you are, Stone, or who came up with the idea! Either one of you could have put a stop to it at any time. The damage wrought by your carelessness is done!

"What Grey and I want to know is what you two knuckleheads thought was gonna happen when ya tried to ride that old cranky, unpredictable longhorn? We certainly wouldn't have climbed on his back!"

Grey broke in and ordered his boys in a stern voice, "Tell your uncle and me what's going through your thick heads? Then I'll tell you what's goin' through ours?"

If eyeballs could peel paint off a wall, then Grey's glare would have left the office needing a fresh coat. The whole story as to what happened this afternoon hadn't come out yet. Grey was trying to hold his temper in check until he could hear it from the beginning.

He knew the girls weren't blameless because those two tomboys never were, but they had to be put to bed with fever, in pain, and under Doc's care. He couldn't ignore the what-if thoughts of how much worse this could have turned out. The boys had to take responsibility and quit including the girls in dangerous behaviors. It was high time for them to grow up!

Stone and Clay wisely kept their mouths shut. They had solemn expressions on their faces. Pa had their attention, and he had a right to be mad at them, and they deserved whatever punishments he imposed.

Grey had a direct question for Stone and Clay.

"This hairbrained notion just popped into your head on the spur of the moment, did it?" He snapped his fingers so loudly; the unexpected sound startled them and even Cole.

"It just popped into your minds, let's ride a cranky, old, longhorn steer today! It'll be easy! It'll be fun! What could possibly go wrong?"

Stone answered, "Uh, no, Sir, I'd been thinking about riding a longhorn for a good, long while, but I'd never planned to involve Sari and Maisy. I figured Clay would go with me because we're always together."

"Wait! Why on earth, did you want to ride a longhorn steer, Stone?"

"Pa, do you remember the man who rode the longhorn steer down front street last year on the 4th of July?"

Both Grey and Cole knitted their eyebrows together and exchanged glances at Stone's question.

"Well, I admired the look of him ridin' on the big, boney steer with those huge horns. It's when I started thinking about trying it myself. Today, when we were hanging around on Frank's Hill shootin' the breeze, I said it out loud."

I said, "I'm gonna try ridin' old Tex."

"The mistake I made was mentioning it in front of the girls. I won't ever do it again! They want to do everything Clay and I try. After the cat was out of the bag, I should have refused to let them go with us.

"I just wanted to see if I could ride Tex in a parade or somewhere.

"When Maisy and Sari decide somethin', it's hard for a man to put his foot down. Women are hard to handle. I thought I made it clear I was the only one gonna do the riden'.

"I have to admit, I expected Tex not to mind me sitting on his back, him being so gentle an' all. This was a miscalculation on my part. He doesn't like it one iota!"

The girls did have a record of getting into trouble. They were stubborn to a fault and had always tried to keep up with Stone and Clay. Their being so headstrong had amounted to several mishaps in the past. However, nothing this serious had ever transpired before!

"Here's the deal, boys, if you see someone ridin' down the road on a longhorn steer, a bull, or even a red heifer, you better think more than twice about the training it took to get the animal to accept a rider! They're not horses.

"What happened today was irresponsible. At least you should have talked it over with me or your uncles!

"The 4th of July longhorn you're rememberin' was most likely trained from the beginning as a bottle calf to make him gentle and tolerant of being handled in close contact with people. Longhorns left to be raised by their mammies grow up to be as wild in their heads as their mamas!

"Tex had no experience with anyone climbing on his back, so he went ornery-crazy with fear and directly set on dislodging your weight! Since the four of you tried, you made him good and mad!"

"Pa," Clay broke in, "This wasn't all Stone's fault. It was my own idea to get up on Tex after Stone was thrown. He didn't have anything to do with my actions. Then, when I got thrown off gettin' the wind knocked out of me, Stone and Maisy tried to help me get to breathing again. Their attention was on me, not Tex or Sari! None of us had an inkling Sari would try and show off.

"While they were bent over me, Sari was up on top of Tex before they knew what she was doin'. She flew through the air and landed face down in a thick patch of goat heads. Then Stone and I concentrated on tryin' to help Sari. Landin' in the goat head patch was bad."

"Yeah, Pa, then while Clay and I were pullin' stickers out of Sari, she was cryin' so hard, well, uh, and you know Maisy, she wasn't about to be outdone by the three of us. She was on Tex in a second."

Stone continued. "Come to think of it, Maisy actually stayed on his back longer than any of us, if it'd been a contest, she won."

This caused Cole to turn his head hiding a grin. Maisy was just like her ma. She wasn't going to play second fiddle to any man.

Cole spoke up sternly, "Yeah, and she got hurt the worst

of any of ya. None of this turned out better or best for anybody, did it? None of you were winners today!"

"Boys," Pa said, "did either of you think even once of Tex's welfare? Your Uncle Smith is out hungry right now with other tired men who haven't filled their bellies with supper yet, rounding up Tex to see if he's hurt. They'll have to mend the fence before they can come back."

The boys made distressed guttural throat noises, and in unison said, "We're sorry Pa and Uncle Cole."

"Sorry isn't enough, boys. You'll be doing the girls' chores while they're healing in addition to your own every day until they feel like working again. In addition, both of your uncles and I will find extra work for all four of you to do since apparently you have too much idle time on your hands.

"Also, each one of you including the girls will owe Uncle Smith and each hand who helped out today two bits. You'll have to earn the money to compensate them for the trouble you've caused.

"In addition, if Tex is too bad hurt, you'll have to put him down which is a miserable job for any man to have to do. Then you'll dig the hole big enough to bury him."

"What do you think, Cole?"

"I think this is settled, and I'm goin' home to eat with my family and check on Maisy." He turned around to leave, but as he was walking out of the room stopped and made an admission.

"Boys, I know how feisty my girl is. She's a handful for sure, but you mark my words. I'm gonna be harder to deal with if you let her get badly hurt again." Then he was gone.

"Yeah, boys, let's go to the kitchen. I've smelled roast beef as long as I can stand it. You're probably hungry as wolves after the trouble you've seen today.

"I agree with your uncle, this business is settled. There'll be no more talk on it."

CHAPTER 5

————— ◆ ◈✦◈ ◆ —————

TERRITORIAL MARSHAL JD STEARNS

What started out as a minor rash of petty crimes had slowly picked up speed and stakes causing uneasiness on the tall grass plains and creating a headache for the territorial marshal, JD Stearns. At first, the reports were of small thefts near and around Spur. Steadily the seriousness and the perimeters of the activities were broadening. The money losses were adding up. Each larceny had one or two details in common with the others, and a trackable pattern was beginning to emerge.

The outlaws, now considered to be a gang, responsible for the reign of fear had to be stopped. People were jumpy as all get-out and on alert for anything seeming out of the ordinary in open country, in surrounding townships, and small obscure settlements. People were watching their stock more carefully, and mayors formed brigades to patrol streets at night. Farmers stayed closer to home, carrying guns into the fields, and leaving their women with ways of protecting themselves and the children.

Tension in the territory had become so thick, it could be cut with a butter knife. At night, many heads of livestock were moved into barns or brought up closer to houses. More care in locking up was taken and some even built wooden shutters to better cover the windows with holes cut to see out and fire guns if necessary. Merchants locked their stores more tightly, guarded their businesses at night, and secured goods more diligently.

No one had been hurt or killed yet, but with guns involved, and the stress level continuing to mount, a real catastrophe happening was becoming more likely. The unidentified thieves were persistent cusses and rapidly escalating their activities. The outlaws were getting bolder and greedier. Their leader hadn't been careless yet, but odds were he'd make a mistake in the law's favor sooner rather than later.

Marshal JD made his home office in Denton County in the town of Spur, Texas. He had two dependable deputies to back him and maintain the peace when he had to be elsewhere in the territory. Within the boundaries JD routinely patrolled, there were several small-town sheriffs with deputies operating in their jurisdictions. They kept the lids fastened down on most troubles, but ocaissionly, JD had to get involved.

The marshal and Texas Ranger Grey Byrd still rode together whenever JD needed more support. Grey's ranch was in Garza County close to Cap Rock. He was semi-retired from duty, but still highly respected for his experiences and successes as a ranger. He and Stearns were good friends and worked well when they put their heads and skills together.

The two were in sync on the trail and trusted each other implicitly. They had a lot of blended history. JD was the reason Grey still kept his badge polished. The marshal requested the State Capitol to offer him a part-time ranger position instead of the retirement he requested. This arrangement allowed the rancher time to be at home with his family and to run Byrd Ranch with his brothers, Smith and Cole.

JD's pa had been a dedicated town sheriff. It ended for him one day when a young kid rode into his province wanting to make a name for himself as a fast gun. JD's pa tried talking him out of drawing, but he couldn't be deterred. The kid must have been practicing for a long while because the bullet left his gun like greased lightning.

In an instant his capable father lay on his back dead in the street. His hand still gripping the handle of his six-shooter which had never completely cleared the holster. His wonderful pa, James Daniel Stearns, was a respected lawman with many friends. The men of the town quickly formed a posse and took out after the killer.

When they caught up with the kid, he hadn't gotten far. He refused to be taken alive to hang and pulled his gun. When it was all over, he went down riddled with six bullets from five different guns. Three of the wounds were each death shots.

At the time, JD still lived at home with ma and pa. He grieved as hard at the loss as any young man who'd just lost his father, the most significant person in the world to him. He appreciated and thanked the townsmen for hunting and killing the gunslinger. He'd looked up to his pa and made the decision to be a good man just like him and become a lawman with his pa's integrity.

He tried his best to continue living in the house with his ma, but the truth was she'd never shown him love or kindness. His pa had run interference between them all of JD's life. After he was gone, she ranted and raved about many things. JD couldn't put together enough of her thoughts to understand what she was trying to say. She spoke in riddles and innuendos.

One day she angrily admitted to JD she'd always truly hated him from the very beginning. She said she'd never asked to raise James's child, but agreeing to accept him was the only way James Daniel would agree to marry her. He took her words to mean she might not be his mother after all.

The very next day, he came home to find all of his things tossed in the yard haphazardly. He gathered a few things important to him from the yard and a few things of his pa's from the house and rode away without even a parting word. He'd never looked back once.

He'd received a telegram when his Ma recently passed, but knowing she was gone meant nothing to him. JD didn't care and hadn't even ridden back to attend the funeral or visit her grave. She was a memory he preferred to keep in the past. As a little boy who needed comfort from a mother, she'd only frightened and hurt him instead. He had nothing to mourn.

One of the guns hanging at JD's hip was the very one his father's hand was wrapped around when he died. It was a reminder of the fine brave man who used it before him. He wore it out of respect. After leaving home, he'd practiced with this weapon of defense until his draw was faster than greased lightning, and his aim was true. Only then did he feel ready to take the badge of a lawman and commit to uphold the rule of the land.

Now, his wife was a special kind of woman, a nurturing wife and mother. He loved his beautiful Lilac completely. Before she came, he'd slogged through the solitary, lonely life of an unloved man. Lilac changed his life. She was his everything.

She completed him and filled in all the blanks with more love and soothing gestures than he'd ever imagined possible. What man could not love a darling woman such as his wife and mother to his children? They had two twin girls, Judy and Hazel, and a third baby would be here sometime before next spring.

The only other family he had was his pa's little sister,

Polly Stearns, but he'd not met her. His ma had spoken ill of her at every opportunity, not hiding the fact she hated her. As a kid, he remembered once seeing a picture of his aunt put on the mantle by his pa. JD had been drawn to her sweet likeness.

His questions and curiosity about the girl in the picture angered his Ma, and she flung it into the woodstove. To this day, the likeness of the pretty girl turning black in the flames was etched in his mind. Pa sent him outside, but he could still hear his parents arguing to this day.

Surprisingly, a few years ago, right out of the blue, he received a post from his mysterious Aunt Polly. It was marked San Antonio. He hadn't known where she lived or how to find her until then. He hadn't known if she was even alive. She signed her last name as Stearns, so evidently, she'd never married. They'd exchanged letters, and she'd offered to find the perfect mail order bride for him. The offer came at a time when he truly desired a wife but had no time to hunt for one himself.

Not too long after, Lilac's first letter arrived, and JD read it dozens of times. It was full of the joy and hope he needed to have in his life so badly. The paper was pink and smelled like roses. He'd slept with it under his pillow for the longest time until he replaced it with her picture.

They shared many missives back and forth over the next year and were married by proxy before she traveled to Spur. He told her not to come join him for a year, so he had time to firmly establish his job and build a house for them. When he finally gave her the go ahead, she arrived soon after. The two officially and publicly married in the church before living together. This had been their plan. He'd fallen head over heels in love with her at first sight.

She shared many interesting stories about Aunt Polly. Lilac described her as a handsome, efficient woman with a lot of sense and an intuitive mind for business. She depicted her as a lady who took guff off of no one. Polly

Stearns sufficiently took care of herself and was more than financially secure. Lilac admired her independent and courageous spirit.

JD was determined to meet his Aunt Polly in person someday. Maybe, he'd take his little family to San Antonio to visit as soon as the new baby was here and old enough to travel. Wouldn't that be something?

CHAPTER 6

POLLY STEARNS

Polly Stearns was a woman willing to work as hard and long as it took to better her circumstances. Injustices and humiliations forced upon her as a child didn't break her spirit but conquering them forged her into the strong-willed person of grit she'd grown to be today.

Having been abandoned twice, she knew how it felt to hit rock bottom and have no one or any resources. With the help of the true God's empathy, she had reached down and pulled herself up by the bootstraps.

Polly started believing in the never-ending power of Jesus who loved her and had been by her side even when she hadn't known He was there. Knowing Him had made her compassionate towards other people who struggled.

Jesus who held the whole world in his hands forgave her and healed the young, broken girl she'd been. He gave her the courage to catch the hard balls before they hit and experience the joy of throwing them back as soft balls full of blessings to those who needed help as she once had.

Polly Stearns was tough as nails and able to face any threat, but her thick skin aside, she was sincerely a good person. Above all else, she loved her son whom she'd never seen, and she was on her way to find him.

Word had reached her of the death of her blackhearted sister-in-law. She was the last thread keeping the truth away from her son. He deserved to know she was his real mother and learn the truth of why she'd stayed out of his life until now.

She'd signed a legally binding order to give her baby up years ago. The death of her brother's widow finally broke the ugly thread making the document null and void. The woman had always stood between Polly and her only child, holding them apart.

She'd made up her mind to travel to the tall grass prairie and put things right with her son, knowing he might not welcome her. Bitterness and hard feelings might be the result of the truth she had to tell JD, but he had a right to know. She prayed JD had a heart soft and open enough to hear her out and accept the decisions she and her brother had hastily made together.

She was praying Lilac would be the oil needed to smooth things over with the son who didn't even know she existed. After all these years of silence, she was determined to step forward.

Bad memories made cruel bedfellows, and sometimes hers revisited in the night. Just a child, she'd allowed a handsome, silver-tongued man to take advantage of her innocence, and it had cost her everything of value.

Her parents were devout members of an extremist religious sect living in a secluded valley called New Harmony. Things were only seen in black or white and from the perspectives of crochety, old men. The valley was ruled by pious self-appointed elders who made up the false church doctrine and inflicted cruel punishments keeping people in line.

By the judgement of men dressed in black with long beards, Polly had sinned against God and was cast out because she could never be redeemed. Cruelly, she was banished without mercy from the only home she'd ever known, and her baby boy was taken from the womb without Polly being allowed to see him.

Little Polly, just fourteen years old, had literally been thrown out the door into the snow as soon as she was able to shakily stand from the birthing bed. Trembling, she was thrust into winter's cold with one threadbare quilt and a loaf of stale bread. She'd beaten on the door until her small hands were battered and bleeding, but no one answered her cries for help.

Broken in body and spirit, she took refuge in the drafty barn to escape the cutting wind. She desperately needed to lie down. She was weak, nauseous, and bleeding between her legs. Her stomach cramped from the delivery. Her older brother, James Daniel, found her there when he came to do the evening chores.

He warned her. "You can't stay here long sister. If Pa discovers you, he'll use the buggy whip on your back. You'll end up in worse shape than you are now. I'll pile up a mountain of straw back in a corner for you to hide behind for a little while. You'll have to plan on leaving on your own strength before I do chores tomorrow night. I can only hide you until then."

"What about my babe, James Daniel?" Polly cried out begging him for help.

"Shhhh! You be still! They will not let you have him, so get it out of your head. He could die with you in winter's freeze anyway. Your only hope to get out of here alive is to leave this place alone. Get out of here if you can and don't look back.

"I've been thinking some on the neighbor girl. She's seventeen and has been pestering me to marry her. I'll tell Ma and Pa tonight I intend to get married as soon as possible and take your son to raise as my own. You know the folks will mistreat him if he stays in Pa's house, and you can trust he'll be safe with me. We've always been able to depend on each other, Polly."

By the next evening, she was gone with a small sack of food and what little money James Daniel could scrape together. She bought passage as far as the money would take her and landed on the streets of San Antonio. A kind man, a doctor, found her exhausted, hungry, cold, and very sick huddled in a doorway. He and his wife took her into their home and nursed her back to health.

They were wonderful people with no children. She stayed with them for several years, working beside the doctor as a nurse, cleaning their house, and doing whatever she could to earn her keep. She gradually learned how to provide for herself and how to use every difficult experience she'd had to teach her something important about herself, people, and survival.

Polly gave her heart to Jesus. She became confident in her thinking, resilient, and refused to repeat mistakes, including falling for another silver-tongued devil like Alex Johns. In fact, she avoided men to protect herself.

Ironically, she accidently fell into her own niche in San Antonio as a match maker. She had a passion for helping women who needed a hand up for whatever reason. Her empathy for other women escalated into a lucrative business helping her and them both.

Society had come to accept the idea of mail order brides as a valid approach to marriage for many varied reasons. Polly Stearns found she had a gift for connecting men and women from all over the country suited to enter into matrimony together. She earned a steady living as an intermediary, a reputable third party. She located prospects, screened them as best she could and paired suitable matches.

Polly got the word out in newspapers, contacted churches, and sent flyers to small settlements in all four geographical directions. Word of her honest dealings and solid reputation spread quickly. Both males and females started contracting her assistance in procuring harmonious marital situations.

Significant population shifts and circumstances across the country increased her business, and the dream of establishing an agency grew. When the war between the states came to an end, far too many husbands, fathers, fiancés, and young boys never made it home. There was a huge shortage of men to go around.

Females left alone needed males to marry and make homes. Mothers needed fathers for children who had lost theirs to fighting for the north or south. Some young women simply needed to escape bad conditions.

All of these ladies had one thing in common, they wanted homes and would gladly move anywhere to avoid the trials of loneliness and destitution. Love didn't matter so much as long as a man and woman were a compatible match and agreed to honor the responsibilities tacked onto marriage. Love might come later, and in many, maybe even most cases it did follow.

Then came the gold rush luring eligible men to relocate west and seek their fortunes. The majority of miners ended up with empty pockets and hands covered in raw blisters, but they'd fallen in love with the beautiful land and its possibilities. Many of them stayed, but they needed wives as homemakers, companions, and for building families. Sending back east for a mail order bride became widely, popular adding to Polly's workload.

In addition, the taming of the Westward expansion called men to claim the free land being offered. Men took the gamble and became pioneers. Some were already married, but many weren't. They gave up the conveniences of civilization and made the dangerous treks to places where women were scarce as hen's teeth. The homesteaders worked hard on their parcels of land to make them produce, and they constructed shelters for living.

A cabin, however, was not a home without a wife to make it into one and provide the chance for subsequent children. Farmers didn't or couldn't spare the time to go back east to find wives for themselves. A fortunate few had connections back east willing to find suitable matches for them, but many relied on the mail to make connections with unattached women willing to trade letters, get acquainted, and consider them as potential husbands.

The demand for mail-order brides and husbands exploded. In order to better handle the flood of new customers, Polly bought a big brick house on a hill in San Antonio, Texas. She hired office help, a cook, and a housekeeper. She turned it into a boarding house of sorts for ladies who were without support and looking for husbands.

Polly began publishing quarterly catalogues of pictures and letters reaching both male and female readers far and wide. A Post Office box number was the only means of contacting her agency with submissions, inquiries, or correspondence. The East to West Mail Order Bride Agency was a booming success.

Since so many bachelors in the West were seeking wives, Polly decided to locate a second branch office in West Texas where many single men wanted wives to tame the west. Deciding to kill two birds with one stone, she made plans to one day establish The West to East Mail Order Bride Agency where her estranged son and his family made their home in Spur, Texas.

The murder of her brother in the line of duty was a shock. Then the recent death of his wife untied Polly's hands. She felt free to finally reach out to JD and claim her son. Actually, over two years ago she'd fudged on her oath and sent a letter to JD Stearns introducing herself as his father's spinster sister and his aunt. These words were only half true.

Surprisingly, he'd sent a note back rather quickly. In her next missive, she told him a bit about her business and offered to find a suitable wife for him. She was surprised once again when he readily agreed to this.

One day the demure, virginal Lilac knocked on her door looking for a husband in the west. Polly just bet she'd found her son's match. The two started exchanging letters. Lilac had no family left or steady work. She accepted the offered room and board from Polly. The girl insisted on paying her own way with light office work and cleaning.

She and Polly grew close, and Polly began teaching her about all the things a good wife needed to know to be a homemaker and how to please her husband. Polly became quite fond of the girl and more invested in saving this particular woman for JD.

To cement a commitment between them, she arranged for JD and Lilac to marry by proxy on paper between her lawyer and JD's legal counsel. A year later, Lilac left for Spur to be married properly in the community church.

Then Polly and Lilac started corresponding back and forth. Polly was hungry for the sweet letters providing a window into her son's and daughter's-in-law lives together.

Lilac had since bore twin girls, Judy and Hazel. Now, she and JD were expecting a third baby. Polly was nervous to tell JD the truth about her identity, but it was the only path to becoming, in some way, a part of their happy family. She was aware her revelation was going to be shocking and had put a lot of thought into the best way to broach the subject.

CHAPTER 7

---※◆❖◆※---

ALL ABOARD!

~ *Polly*

Polly's abbreviated childhood and the unfair indignances handed out by abusive parents made her appreciate special life-moments more than most. Today was a new beginning. She was leaving before daybreak from San Antonio for the chance to connect with her son and restart her life.

She also faced the trip ahead with excitement but also trepidation. While maintaining the outward appearance of composure, she felt like a fish out of water flopping on the bank. Traveling wasn't something she'd experienced except the one time she'd traveled from New Harmany to San Antonio. She'd only been fourteen. Standing in line to board the train was intimidating. She could imagine herself stepping off into deep water and struggling to find the bottom.

The black behemoth had grown in size the closer it had

approached the depot and to the place she was standing. Now it looked and sounded like an iron monster. She was startled by the loud bursts of steam expelling from the top of its tall stack, the metal wheels screaming against the rails as it rolled to a stop, and the unsavory odors it belched.

A porter stepped out of an open door. He was dressed in a black suit accented with ribbons, medallions, and rows of brass buttons. A snappy visor cap shadowed the upper portion of his face. The diminutive man set out a small wooden riser for boarders to use as a step up making it easier to reach the actual train steps.

Ripples of greetings and farewells came from behind her on the station's platform. Some passengers were here to board while others were departing the train from another door. Polly, the novice voyager, had little idea what lay ahead of her on this trek. She'd not ventured out into the world except through books and the hundreds of letters exchanged between lonely people who'd never met.

By noon, it became clear to her being a passenger in a packed train car was uncomfortable and monotonous. It was no longer exciting. The confines of the narrow car were oppressive. The first leg of her journey from San Antonio to Abilene was arduous.

Before leaving, she had read a good horse could travel approximately twenty miles a day in good weather. In comparison a locomotive could cover twenty miles in one hour. In reality, she now knew the reported speed of a train was entirely exaggerated.

The many stops and starts along the track to load and unload freight, drop passengers off, and wait for new ones to board had a ravenous appetite for eating up time. Polly began to wonder if she shouldn't have opted to ride the horse!

This is when it occurred to her a railroad line operated on profits like any other business. While railroads made their reputations moving people, they made the real money moving freight. The supreme goal was to generate as much cash revenue per run as possible.

Big money did not come from the selling of individual tickets and accommodating travelers. It was made by moving cattle for beef, pigs for pork, sheep for mutton, horses, chickens, raw materials, commercial goods, farm products, and US Mail contracts.

It took time to load and unload these money makers. Sizable amounts of fuel and water were required to keep the heavy steam locomotive powered. Coal bins and water tanks had to be replenished from sky-high water towers located along the way. These refills took time.

Time was also allotted allowing travelers to stretch their legs, use the railroad line's facilities, and to buy sandwiches, hand pies, fruits, vegetables, containers of water, and handmade items from vendors waiting to sell to passengers.

Polly understood how this venue supplemented the incomes of people living in outlying areas. These sellers were common, hardworking people who depended on this market to supplement their small farms and living expenses. She admired the women in bonnets of all ages for taking advantage of this opportunity to earn a few extra coins for their families.

There were other inconveniences traveling the rail besides time losses. Horrific noises, abrupt jolts, and continuous jostling made muscles sore and achy. Each stop and start sounded like cars buckling together with reverberations of metal jammed against metal. Ear piercing, whistle blasts, and the monotonous undertones of iron wheels rubbing against iron tracks were horrific.

There was a steady mechanical rhythm beating a repetitive clackety-clack, clackety-clack, clackety-clack. Polly found it somewhat mesmerizing as the train moved forward at a steady clip. Sleeping on the train was impossible for Polly, but she did doze occasionally in a trans-like state of mind.

Putrid smells assaulted her olfactory system with black smoke clouds produced by burning coal. They were continually burped by the smokestack. Inhaling drew the polluted air into the lungs. Ash and black carbon made a mess of everything it reached.

The blowback of sooty cinders pulled into the car through open windows covered clothing and belongings with grime and on occasion left small burn holes in cloth. Polly was seriously considering throwing the clothing she wore away instead of trying to clean it.

The acrid smells induced choking, raw throats, and coughing fits. Women and men alike held handkerchiefs to their mouths and noses trying to filter their breaths. Cowboys lay back with hats covering their faces. They appeared to be sleeping, but how could sleep be possible in such an environment?

A mixed bag of people sat in Polly's car with an array of differences. Polly catalogued them as clean, dirty, well-dressed, poorly dressed, loud, quiet, old, and young. Cowboys were easy to spot wearing wide-brimmed hats, sharp-toed boots, spurs, bandanas, and sporting side arms.

There were also farmers and laborers wearing denims, work boots, and straw hats. Some passengers were alone or in small groups. A few young families grappled to keep children entertained and bribed with snacks.

Mannerly decorum seemed to be pushed to the back burner by many. She'd never heard so much belching, farting, and spitting in her entire life. Some galoots who chewed tobacco couldn't hit the spittoons to save their lives. Other men smoked cheroots, cigarettes, and pipes letting the ashes fall to the floor.

The old woman sitting by Polly carried a live chicken with a string of red yarn tied around its neck. The hen was sitting on there like it was used to traveling, for heaven's sake! One old farmer even had a noisy little goat standing at his feet, nibbling anything he could reach.

Squalling children had to be calmed periodically, usually to no avail. People talked loudly, sometimes even yelling at one another to be heard over the clatter and commotion of the train. Polly noticed many had given up trying to visit miles back.

It would seemed like hours before pulling into the Abilene station in the midafternoon. It was the end of the train ride for Polly Stearns.

Freight cars were unloaded and reloaded as usual, and passengers boarded and departed headed in the direction of Fort Worth. Abilene and Fort Worth were both cattle towns. Ranchers herded and transported their cattle from every direction to be bought. The buyers shipped them east where the appetite for beef was enormous, and the pockets were just as deep.

From here, a stagecoach was the only mode of transportation besides horses for those going farther into West Texas. Polly would be on it. An Overland Stage flat-bed wagon waited to collect mail bags, light freight, baggage, and passengers. The stagecoach line subsidized its income with profitable US Mail contracts and often transported raw gold or freshly minted US coins ready for circulation.

Passengers were charged ten cents a mile to travel by stage. Public transportation was again all about the almighty dollar lining the pockets of the already rich. To the front of the large, open-air wagon were three anchored wooden benches for transporting passengers to the Overland Stage Line Office in the middle of town.

Stepping inside the dusty stage office really drove home the realization Polly had left the cushy life she'd built behind. Standing behind the ticket counter, a scowling, wrinkled faced man with a physique comparable to a skeleton wore a black visor making his sandy, lack-luster hair poof out above it and stick out jaggedly beneath it.

The long, dingy sleeves of his once white pinstriped shirt were supported under his shoulders by black arm garters. He offered neither words of greeting nor words of encouragement as he took cash in exchange for tickets rubber-stamped with destinations.

Outside an equally detached man gathered the tickets and ordered the passengers belongings tossed roughly on top of the coach to be tied down. Other workers were busy stuffing mail bags into the scuffed leather boot on the back of the huge Concord. Polly didn't miss the heavy, locked canvas bag being stashed in a wooden box under the driver's perch.

A striking older gentleman took command of the waiting group just by his mere presence. His thick wavy hair came almost to his shoulders. It was dark charcoal with stripes of gray, and his face had short whiskers topped off with a well-groomed handlebar mustache.

Polly tried not to stare, but she didn't often see a man who struck her fancy. In fact, she could even say she'd never seen such a man. Twenty-seven years ago, she'd been duped by a handsome man, and she hadn't looked at one since.

"Name's Kriss, I'll be your driver, and make no mistake, I'll give the orders on this trip, and you'll obey them. If I say to jump, you can only ask how high. Otherwise, keep yer mouths shut!"

Why did he look at me when he said this?

"There will be no second-guessing me. What I say might save yer life." He held Polly's gaze longer than necessary until she finally looked away.

"Do whatever I tell ya to do, no arguments."

Then he started barking out directions to follow.

"Eat hearty here folks and be back ready to board in thirty minutes. The stage won't wait fer stragglers. This is the last chance you'll have to pick up extra sandwiches and such. I suggest ya include a couple of jars of water for the trip and visit an outhouse before we leave.

"The overnight relay station does have water and sells food, but ya may not like it. Doesn't hurt to have a few victuals with ya in case something happens, and ya need 'em. Hope it's not the case, but we might break down."

For heaven's sake! Would it crack his face to smile?

Polly didn't appreciate this man's attitude, and opened her mouth to say as much when he turned his back on her and walked across the street to the saloon. It was just as well she didn't have a chance to blurt out what she was thinking.

It wouldn't be worth it to get off on the wrong foot with the driver. Besides she wouldn't have to put up with this Kriss fellow for long. Afterwards, she'd never see the silver fox with the handlebar moustache again. She'd be in Spur, and he'd be long gone.

She had spotted a little café as they passed it on the way to the stage office. Polly made her way there as quickly as her short legs would carry her. She grabbed a small table for two covered in a red and white checked oil cloth. It looked and felt a little greasy to the touch, but it was free of crumbs at least.

On the wall was a sign reading both chili and breakfast were served all day. Chili sounded good, but she was concerned it wouldn't sit well on her stomach. She ordered two eggs over easy, fried potatoes, biscuits, and peppered gravy with coffee instead.

Complying with the silver fox's orders, she also asked the waitress to fix a sack of two ham sandwiches, fruit, cookies, and a jar of water to take with her on the stage. She had no inkling of the trials lying ahead between here and Spur, or she might have asked for a bigger sack.

~Kriss

Kriss bellied up to the bar in the Lazy Susan Saloon. "Jed, pour me a beer." He slapped his dime so hard on the counter it made a little dent.

"What's wrong with you, Friend? Ya look like you're mad enough to bite a ten-penny nail in two! You're getting' ready to pull out on a run, aren't ya?"

"Well, aren't you a man of questions today, Jed. I don't know which one to answer first. Yeah, I'm leavin' in a half hour with a full load."

"Some cowboy made ya mad already?"

"No, some woman."

"Ohhh, I get it."

"You don't get nothin'. She just reminded me of someone. Give me another beer and mind your own business!"

CHAPTER 8

PILE INTO THE CONCORD

A Concord was the giant of all stagecoaches, and in its glory days, this particular Concord must have been a deluxe used in some city. The worn-out vehicles were demoted to the wild west to live out their days. The once garish, red paint covering the body of this coach had faded in the sun, and the equally dull gold scrolling designs spoke of age and neglect.

The chipped yellow spokes of the big wheels were a testament to the many miles this old girl had rolled. For being forgotten after her hard service and turned out to pasture, she was still sturdy enough to do her job on the prairie.

The fate of Concords was irreversible. As trains and other more modern conveyances replaced the need for stagecoaches and horse drawn buses back east, many were downgraded to dry, dusty West Texas and other desolate places to live out whatever life was left in them. They were abandoned in the name of progress to less populated areas.

The large, bloated body of this whale of a conveyance was suspended on thick leather braces and metal pieces with the driver's roost attached directly on the top right side in front. This ensured the driver had nearly the same benefits of the suspension system as passengers riding inside the coach.

Lighter built coaches with all metal and wood supporting them bounced along roughly from one side to the other over rocks and uneven ground. A Concord provided an easier, front to back rocking motion resulting in a smoother, more comfortable ride.

When Polly returned from eating, a team of six muscled horses had been hitched to the loaded coach. Each animal had its own set of reins controlled by the driver. A skilled handler could hold all twelve ribbons with his left hand leaving his right hand to work the brake. He could give any individual horse in the team a message of correction. Controlling a team this large took practice to master and quite a bit of skill.

The man who was introduced as Charlie Shotgun, rode to Kriss's left and would stay on the lookout for trouble. Since the body of the Concord rested extra-high over the tall wheels, the distance to the ground from the top of the conveyance was quite a drop. Anyone on top could fall to their deaths if bullets or arrows didn't kill them first.

The once pristine hickory trim of this Concord's box was accented with brass doodads formed by craftsmen. Inside the coach were three rows of wooden seats, anchored to the bed. Two faced forward toward the front and the third row was placed in front against the front wall facing toward the back. This meant nine passengers could fit inside and two more could hitch a ride up top with the baggage.

Musty, oiled canvases hung over the open windows but offered scant shelter from the elements. They didn't keep much of the dust, heat, and cold out but blocked the sun and kept snow and rain out fairly well. To catch a breeze or see the scenery, the fabric could be rolled up and tied out of the way.

On this run there were eight passengers. Two of them were cowboys armed with pistols, rifles, and carrying their saddles. They chose to ride on top with their gear in the open air. The cowpokes were brothers named Cecil and Stan and evidently preferred their own company.

Polly suspected they liked their vices and probably wanted to be free to swig whiskey, smoke, cuss, or spit tobacco juice. Polly had always envied men their freedoms. She didn't use tobacco or cuss much, but she felt privileges given to men in comparison to those of women were quite unfair.

In rebellion, she carried an initialed, silver whiskey flask, a loaded pepper-pot revolver dropped into her deep skirt pocket, and a slender knife hidden in the lining of her boot. She was trained with a rifle too, but a rifle was hard to conceal.

Polly and a deathly thin girl with honey-colored hair were the only females. They sat together in the front row of seats facing four men. This location gave Polly the chance to keep her eyes on them. Since she didn't know who they were, she didn't trust them as far as she could throw them.

Two men sat on each row. She figured one to be a card shark. She'd learned to spot professional gamblers in San Antonio. Another wore a scuffed bowler and a dusty suit. A pad of dog-eared paper and a couple of lead pencils could be seen sticking out of a suit pocket. She pegged him for a drummer. There was a man dressed in denim work clothes and a straw hat like a farmer or homesteader might wear.

The fourth man was short, plump, almost bald-headed, and fidgety. He could not sit still. His jerky movements and two large front teeth reminded her of a large, buck-toothed squirrel. His pressed, brown suit was free of dust, and his shoes were polished to a shine. A heavy, gold watch chain draped from his thick leather belt and disappeared up into a vest pocket.

This man avoided making eye contact with anyone or exchanging words. He was as nervous as a tomcat in a room full of rocking chairs. Stranger than all these details put together was the tightly wedged leather bag on the floor between his feet. It had a shiny lock under the handle. Without solid justification, Polly instantly disliked this squirrely, little man.

Right on time, just as Kriss had threatened, he slammed and latched the doors and in moments, the coach rocked abruptly forward and then back again with only a jolt. After two or three hours of this rocking back-and-forth motion, Polly was a little nauseous and definitely over-heated. Her entire body was sore, drained of its usual starch, and she felt the fatigue of the terribly long day.

Thankful, she didn't have coal dust, smoke, or gritty cinders plaguing her, she counted her blessings one by one. She prayed the driver would go faster and cover the miles ahead quickly. She heard Kriss yell, "Whoa, whoa!" in his deep velvety voice. She knew God had heard her prayer, and they were stopping for the night.

A sweaty Kriss opened the door and released his prisoners. She got a scent of him. It was all man, soap, spice, and whiskey. Once they were standing outside, he barked.

"We'll only be at this relay station for thirteen minutes, just long enough to switch the tired team for a fresh one. Stretch yer legs and take care a yer business out back of the building."

He made eye contact with Polly, before he yelled, "You females find a good-sized stick and stay together, keep the stage in sight, and watch out for rattlers. A rattler don't care who he bites, and he bites to kill! You'd be dead in less than a half-hour!

"All ya'll listen up now. When I whistle, you'll have

three minutes to board. I got a schedule to keep, you know, so don't take advantage! It would be unpleasant to be stranded here until the next stage comes through!"

Polly was so worn out, she was thinking like a spoiled child, but dang if she didn't hate the whiskered silver fox with tobacco juice dried on his chin. It was so easy to target her petulance directly at this bully.

Of course, she was being unfair, but still, she'd like to shoot him with her revolver. Maybe she might when they reached Spur. It didn't hurt anything to think about it.

As soon as the thought of murder crossed her mind, she immediately asked God to forgive her. This man was rough and stern, but he had a job to do. Probably, no one would listen to him if he wasn't mean. This desolate country was untamed and dangerous. Anything could happen.

"Driver, excuse me. When do you expect us to arrive in Spur?"

He stared for a long moment making Polly regret she'd asked the question, but she didn't shrink. He turned his head slightly and spit a small stream of tobacco juice just missing one of her boots before answering. She felt insulted by the gesture.

"We're clipping the miles off right well, are you gettin' worn down so soon, Ma'am? Better get used to hardships piling up like a cord of stove wood out here, Lady. This ain't the city.

"West Texas is brutal on soft ladies not used to hard work. There's no easy livin' on the prairie, it's unforgivin'. I haven't known of purty ones like you to last long here."

Polly had not missed the disdain in his scathing words. He looked her up and down, and she felt like a head of livestock.

"Just lookin' at you, I'd reckoned you to be a fancy, particular lady with soft hands, and quick to take offense. I'd bet a month's wages you've never done a lick a work in your life. You'll be more trouble than your worth out here, absolutely no help to any man, you'll be a liability! Women like you can get a good man killed. I'll warrant you're in for trouble. This prairie's not a ladies' society!"

"How dare you judge me, Mr. Mighty Wagon Master. You know nothing about me. You have no right to talk to address me like this! I promise you I'm tougher and more determined than I look. I'll be around to meet your stage every time it pulls into Spur!"

Polly's words were crisp and clipped. The disagreeable man had the gall to laugh. He laughed at her. She drew her hands into fists by her sides and stood as tall as she could.

"I think I hate you, you, you grizzled old man!"

"Mmmm, well at least you are feisty 'n' got a hot temper. You're gonna need it and all the spit 'n' vinegar you kin muster! Keep your dander up, an' you might survive better than I figure."

Dismissing her, he turned his back and walked off. He tossed these last words of orders at her without turning around, "You better get a move on, little lady, or I'll drive off an' leave ya where you're standin'."

Polly Stearns' face was hot with rage. She was livid, but she was also bone tired. She made up her mind to waste no more energy on this brute. She'd be shed of him soon.

Damn you! If you only knew what I'd give for a hot, soapy bath and a clean feather bed right now, you'd swear you were right about me! I'll show you what I'm made of and get the last laugh!

CHAPTER 9

OVERNIGHT RELAY STATION

The trail had become rougher than Polly had anticipated. The horses were spent, and Polly was near exhaustion as well. The last stop of the day was the overnight relay station. When the Concord pulled in, the cowboys riding on top climbed down quickly to help unhook the team and lead them to water.

This is where Kriss said they'd lay over for the night.

"Be ready to pull out before daybreak in the mornin' or you'll not have a ride."

The sun was just slipping down low on the western horizon. Polly felt like she could sleep standing up. Just the thought of getting up tomorrow sounded impossible.

Two rickety outhouses at the back of the station stood several feet apart. One was leaning farther sideways than the other. Polly claimed one of them, leaving the second for the men. What a far piece she'd strayed from civilization! She was ashamed of how spoiled and lazy she'd become living high on the hog.

The smell of rot and decay emitted by the outhouse was sickening. She wondered if someone had died in there. There was no word in her vocabulary harsh enough to describe the stench. Engorged flies relentlessly swarmed around her face and got tangled around in her hair buzzing frantically trying to get loose.

Polly cracked the creaky door open just a fraction and immediately heard the buzzing of the angry hornets she'd disturbed. She wanted to walk a distance away and squat in the tall prairie grass. It was very tempting until Kriss's warning earlier about rattlesnakes repeated itself in her mind.

Food for supper, if one could call it food, was spread out on a long splintery table. Mismatched wooden bowls were stacked precariously by a pot of gray-colored bean soup and a dented tin can of unmatched spoons. Crusty-looking biscuits and a pan of yellow cornbread were set out. Lard on a plate substituted for butter. Flies, lots of flies, were everywhere! Polly didn't even want to think of where they'd been.

To top it all off, there was an old metal bucket of water and one community dipper. A crude sign marked in black on an old shingle read, '2 Bits'.

Polly's stomach turned over in revolt at the thought of eating or drinking anything from this table. She didn't want to give Kriss any more reason to think he'd been right about her, but this food, this place, was absolutely past the limit of her tolerance. She watched the girl now standing by her eyeing the supper.

If Polly had to guess she'd say this girl didn't have the two bits or even a cent to her name to buy this garbage. By the looks of her worn dress, cracked boots, and the calluses on her hands, she was poor as a church mouse and in some kind of trouble. She looked longingly at the food on the table.

Polly's compassion kicked in reminding her to be kind. *What would Jesus do? He'd feed her.*

She reminded Polly of the homeless, desperate, sick little girl she'd been a long time ago. Polly Stearns remembered exactly how she'd felt being all alone in the world, cold, sick, and hungry.

"Come with me. What's your name?"

In a voice hardly loud enough to hear, she answered, "Martha Wheatley, Ma'am."

"Well, Martha, I'm happy to make your acquaintance. My name is, uh, Melody Potter. I have fresher food on the coach and will be happy to share it with you. Since the sun's gone down, it will be nice with the doors open and the breeze blowing through. The cowboys set up camp outside and have their cookfire going. We'll be safe enough with them around."

Rustic-types, cowhands, wranglers, and such who always seemed to be in need of a haircut and shave had a look. Why Polly would trust these two young cowboys and not Kriss, she had no explanation. Except, Cecil and Stan were boys, and the driver had made her mad enough to spit. But she got the idea a woman would be safe with him.

She'd fallen for a handsome, brawny cowboy once when she was innocent, and it had been the worst mistake of her life. He was a silver-tongued devil who stroked her hair and promised to get her all the things she desired in life.

Instead, the devil lied and lured her. As soon as he had sated his fleshly appetite a few times, he disappeared without a word leaving her to deal with the consequences all alone. He left a baby, a son, behind who belonged to him as much as to her. He threw them away. He didn't keep either of them safe.

Melody Potter was the alias she had decided to use before she left San Antonio. Everyone on her payroll knew to use it until further notice because JD couldn't find out her real name until she was ready.

So, Melody Potter opened her tapestry tote and pulled out two thick ham sandwiches. The waif-thin child glared at them with large, puppy-dog eyes.

"Girl, how long has it been since you last ate? Oh, never mind, Martha, tell me your story while we eat our supper together."

Between bites, chewing, and appreciative moans, Martha Wheatley quietly recounted how she'd wound up here with Polly on this stagecoach. She was a mail order bride. Polly squinted her eyes at her in doubt, knowing she was nowhere near old enough for such a thing.

"How old are you?"

"I just turned fourteen. I've never been away from home or on a stage until today. I'm scared."

"I understand how you feel, child, believe me, I do."

The confession brought back such painful memories for Polly. Martha's ma was just as cruel as her own had been. Both mothers shamed themselves. She had been turned away and robbed of her infant. Martha's ma had sent her beautiful girl-child to a man she didn't know.

It was a despicable thing, but no more contemptable than her own ma and pa did to her when she was Martha's age. They turned her out in the cold of winter when she was fourteen and only hours after she'd given birth to a baby. The very thought of the past made her hunger disappear. She wrapped the half-eaten sandwich back in the waxed paper and returned it to the tote with the rest of the food she'd bought in Abilene.

"Tell me more, Girl. I want to know about your family."

"I'm the oldest of seven children. I can't remember when food was plentiful enough to take away the hunger. Pa made me work in the field along with my brothers. I worked as hard as I could, but nothing I did pleased him.

"It was always something gone wrong, some bad piece

of luck keeping us down, pushing us down harder. It either didn't rain, or it rained too much. Crows picked the seeds up as fast as they were planted or ate the tiny, tender sprouts as soon as they broke through the ground.

"Pests ate the vegetables in the small garden every year. The milk cow dried up, a fox got in the henhouse, and the plow horse went lame. Like I said, it was just one bad thing after another.

"Two months ago, on the day I turned fourteen, Ma told me I had to leave because I was old enough to get married and let someone else pay my way. I couldn't believe she was serious, but she reached into her pocket and handed me a torn newspaper advertisement. The man was looking for a farm wife to do the chores and cook. She stood over me at the table and told me what to write as I cried. I prayed there'd be no return answer.

"Unfortunately, an envelope arrived, and Ma got to the Post Office first, or I would have hidden it. Ed Schmidt from Spur, Texas sent money to buy a ticket on the stage. He'd scribbled words on dirty paper warning me not to cheat him, or he'd make me sorry I ever lived.

"My ma bought me the ticket and told me to wait for the Overland Stage on the day you showed up to board. The dress I'm wearing came out of the missionary box at the church because I didn't own one. The boots on my feet are too small and coming apart. They're the ones I wore in the field."

Polly said, "Let me see the palms of your hands, Martha."

Indeed, the girl did have the broken nails and calluses over calluses she'd earned from her time spent as a field hand, a slave really. Martha had eaten the last bite of her sandwich and the crumbs. Polly handed her a red apple and a large, thick cookie.

She felt empathy toward this fragile girl and disgust for the wicked parents who'd abandoned her. They'd kicked this pretty, defenseless child out the door, and sent her away. This was too much like her own story, and it saddened Polly.

A few things were clear. Ed Schmidt planned to work this child to death, he'd get her pregnant, and he'd abuse her. There was now one less mouth to feed at home, and nobody there cared where she was tonight or wondered how she'd make out. This Ed Schmidt could be an old drunk, a thief, or mean as a snake. It only mattered to them Martha was gone.

With tears rolling down her shallow cheeks, Martha confessed again she was afraid.

Polly said, "I already have a room rented at Mabel's Boarding House in Spur. My associate, Vella, is already there. You're going to stay with us until we figure out how best to help you. You can be sure we'll keep you safe, fed, and out of the hands of this unscrupulous man. I promise you things are going to work out, Martha. I'll let no one hurt you."

Polly passed Martha the water jar and told her they'd better get some rest. She assured her they weren't going back to those filthy outhouses again. She'd make sure they got up before daylight in the morning to relieve themselves in the grass.

CHAPTER 10

◆ ◈✦◈ ◆

THE DAY HELL BROKE LOOSE

Blazing high overhead like a great ball of fire, the sun's heat was bearing down. Polly Stearns, or Melody Potter, depending on the person asking, was unaccustomed to being exposed to such intense heat. She swore the Concord coach was an oven hot enough to bake bread. A real danger of being cooked alive had seriously crossed her mind. The window canvases were rolled and tied to allow the wind's velocity to sweep it through the coach, but for all the effort, the hot as fire gusts provided little relief.

She'd quit worrying about her fellow passengers several miles back. Polly only shared the water jar she'd bought in Abilene with Martha, and it was bone dry now. It was every man for himself, except for her little adopted Martha. She was saving a piece of fruit and two cookies to give the girl later.

Polly removed the ridiculous hat she was wearing and flung it out the open window to blow away and land somewhere downwind. In no time, her usually well-groomed hair popped out of the pins and was flying around her head in a total state of disarray with wisps across her face and getting trapped inside her mouth if she opened it.

She gave up trying to keep it out of her eyes and braided it in a long untidy rope to hang down her back. Martha's hair was displaced and tangled reminding Polly of a bird's nest made of straw. Feeling motherly, Polly cut a piece of cording from a window canvas tie using the thin knife stored in her boot. She tamed the girl's mane by finger-combing and gathering it into a thick tail at the base of her neck. She used the cord to tie it securely.

Polly didn't care a flip about proper etiquette right now as its rules seemed totally impractical on this turbulent West Texas prairie. Scandalously unfastening the top two buttons of her shirtwaist, she daringly pulled her full skirt up to her knees giving a strategic advantage to any possible relief the hot wind could offer.

A lacey, French handkerchief meant for nothing more than a fancy accessory was wadded tightly in the palm of her hand. The thin, translucent square of useless frippery was damp and clammy from wiping her face and neck repeatedly. It had soured and smelled terribly.

What I wouldn't give for a big bandana like Cecil and Stan wear. When I get to Spur, I'm buying a red one!

Her body was beginning to have a ripe aroma, but the others aboard were aromatic as well. The wind's bluster let up occasionally, so every once in a while, she'd get a whiff of underarm odor.

To make the ride even more dreadful, the trail had deteriorated to a rocky and dangerously narrow path. It caused the stage to noisily creak and shake like it might be coming apart. On the left side of the Concord, the rolling grass plains grew as tall-as-a-man, and hemmed them in. It stretched out as far as the eye could see.

The wind rippled it about in great rolling waves like the

ocean currents described in books. Surely the fluidity of this sea of grass and the deep oceans with their waves of water had much in common. Watching the expanse of the rolling, multi-colored grass was captivating.

The right side of the coach was hemmed in by a ragged, sharply broken edge of a great sandstone break. Menacingly, uneven, vicious-looking formations made the canyon below look fierce and formidable. Polly's stomach took a dive each time she looked across the wide mouth of the deep divide. A person could drop to a gruesome death here. She tried to keep from looking down, but the crevasse taunted and called to her.

The ravine could swallow them whole in one bloody gulp. The thought of the stagecoach free-falling into the air end-over-end amid a tangle of horses and hooves with the coach doors sprung open was too much to bear. The picture of the passengers tumbling out like floppy ragdolls brought a dip in her stomach and burning bile up into her throat. Just the thought of what could happen had her heart beating in her chest like a parade drum.

She felt Kriss slowing the Concord considerably, letting the team pick its own way. Horses were capable of choosing the safest paths. This team had traveled this same route many times before and remembered intuitively where to put their feet.

She hoped it was the case because one misstep by a horse might pull the whole team and the conveyance over the wall of rock. Martha reached out to grasp Polly's hand. The girl's hand was trembling, and Polly could see big tears rolling down both cheeks.

Polly took great pity on her and squeezed the hand she held, realizing she was Martha's lifeline. Polly held on tightly, cursing the callus mother who'd sent her beautiful daughter on a dangerous fool's errand.

I'm frightened too, Sweetheart, but any old port in a storm as the sailors say.

Since Kriss slowed the horses down, Polly studied and stared at the view, spellbound by the amazingly vivid and beautiful contrasting shades of light and dark. Red sandstone against the whites and tans was dramatic. In some places on the other side of the ravine, shelves looked wide enough for a man to stand. Sunlight played on the cracks, crannies, and faces of the rough rocks creating mystical shadows.

Each person in the Concord remained perfectly still, stiff, and quiet as if any motion inside the coach could tip the balance. Polly swallowed back as the burning acid from her stomach threatened to strangle her.

Unexpectedly a rifle blast from above the roof pierced the wind. Kriss cursed, loudly, urging the team to go faster, and the cracks of his whip were repeated over and over above the horses' heads. Another shot sounded an exclamation.

The passengers were startled, hollering, or screaming in reaction. Several shots rang out from behind the Concord. Polly could feel the impacts more than hear the poundings of the horses' hooves. The animals were running full-out.

Please Lord, this can't be happening!

Polly Stearns didn't have to be told the stage was under attack, and they could soon be picked off like prey. This was a tense situation developing in real time. Returned blasts from Charlie Shotgun, Cecil, and Stan resonated above her head. The onslaught of fire from the ambushers kept sounding closer.

Without warning, the unmistaken splintering of hickory wood, simultaneously correlated with a bullet ripping through the back of the coach. It entered the head of the man wearing the bowler hat. The velocity of the hit propelled his body forward, dislodging the hat. In horror, her eyes followed a bloody forehead coming down in slow motion to land in her lap.

The sight of blood, the smell of it, and the sickening

weight of his lifeless head forced a series of involuntary screams from her mouth. Without coherent thought, she shoved the man abruptly to the floor. The lifeless body hit profoundly causing his head to bounce on impact. The drummer's order pad and pencils were still seated in his pocket, but he would never pull them out again.

The chilling experience seemed surreal as Polly replayed the horror in her mind. It was too much to process and left her momentarily frozen. Martha squalled and sobbed hysterically beside her. The desperation in the ceaseless noise snapped Polly back to reality. Polly had responsibilities and knew she had to think clearly. Everything was quickly going to hell in a handbasket! This day would be another one she'd never forget, if she lived.

The frightened horses were running helter-skelter at a frenzied stampede. The back wheel on her side of the coach lost purchase and slipped off the jagged side of the trail. The horrific jolt was terrifying and as loud as powerful thunder.

The scraping against rock made her think they surely were destined to topple over the edge into the abyss. She could hear loosened rocks falling down the wall of the ravine. Everyone at the same time hit the floor in a pile trying to save themselves.

The tilt of the coach caused Polly to claw and scurry like an animal until she made it to the top of the dead drummer's body. It didn't dawn on her to whom she was clinging.

The momentum of the coach combined with the unnatural power of the freaked horses must have pulled the compromised weight of the coach enough to purchase solid ground. The wheel had broken completely off leaving the Concord no choice but to lean precariously at an angle. It continued to be drug along the hard ground like a child's toy, but all at once the deafening scraping noise was silenced.

Thankfully, the path had widened, and the winded team had provided enough inertia to keep the stage in motion until it was safe. Kriss's hollering at the team stopped. She would never think disrespectful thoughts of this brave and capable man ever again!

The passengers lay boneless from shock and were compacted into a pile. One last, lone gunshot sounded from the roof. In the turmoil of trying to survive, Polly had selfishly forgotten all the men above her head weathering the attack in the open. She was sure Charlie Shotgun had fallen to his death some time ago. She'd felt a wheel thump and bump over his body, and his gun was silenced. This was to be the valiant man's final trip.

Kriss was silent now, and how she wished to hear him shouting orders at her again. The horsemen in pursuit had pulled their mounts to a stop beside the coach. The desperate race was over, and it seemed evil had won. She prayed harder than she'd ever prayed in her whole life.

The broken whale's body sat motionless. All the noise stopped except for the constant howling of the West Texas wind, and the heaving of horses laboring to breathe. One suffering animal was squealing in pain.

CHAPTER 11

FROM BAD TO WORSE

Martha lay on the floor of the coach where she'd fallen and intermittently sobbed and sniffled heartbreakingly like a child. The male passengers had only just begun to lift their heads cautiously. Polly sat herself up knowing her best bet was to shake off fear and be alert for possibilities.

She quickly ran through a short list of weapons at her disposal starting with the pepperbox revolver in her skirt pocket. It had to be saved for just the right moment because the cylinder only held three rounds. She had more bullets in the pocket, but whoever these villains were, they weren't going to call a time out for her to reload.

The slender, sharp as a razor knife was in the lining of her boot, but it wouldn't be easy to get to it. How stupid Polly felt for sticking the long, sharp hatpin back into her hat before throwing it out the window. She'd reseated it out of habit, but it was a very shortsighted mistake.

She surveyed the inside of the stage, but there wasn't

much of anything to use for fighting. She'd have to fall back on her ingenuity and stall for time. Maybe she'd think of something, or the bandits might make a mistake.

Defensively, she and the other passengers were at a disadvantage unless Kriss and the cowboys above were still able to shoot. She had her doubts about the courage of the men traveling with her, and she doubted any of them were armed. She hoped and prayed to be proven wrong.

The outlaws had played the first hand, and it was violent proof they'd stop at nothing. Soon, she'd be face-to-face with the opponents. Polly couldn't let them see she was a fighter until there was a chance to benefit from showing her grit.

Someone was yelling at the driver and a cowboy to throw down their guns and the money bag stowed under the seat. Since he shouted cowboy instead of cowboys, she figured one of the brothers was dead. A small shower of weapons rained down from above hitting the ground. At the same time, she heard the leather boot on the back of the Concord being ripped open.

Kriss must have had an extra gun stowed under his seat because he fired and was instantaneously shot twice. It sounded like the bullets from an outlaw's gun had hit their target. She heard Kris fall onto the board floor of his perch. It made her incredibly sad to think he was probably dead.

"You, cowboy! Start pitching down the baggage and freight! Then, climb down!

She could hear the outlaws scrambling to dodge the bags as they started falling.

"Careful, Cowboy, you son-of-a-bitch, or I'll shoot you now."

Only one of the doors on the leaning Concord was accessible. It was suddenly yanked open without warning by a muscular man wearing a light brown Stetson. His face was completely covered except for the eyes, and he looked ludicrous.

He was appraising the passengers before making eye contact with Polly. He stared straight at her. She raised her chin slightly and stared right back at him. She couldn't resist showing defiance.

He laughed at her harmless indignation and willfulness.

"Well, ain't ya a sight for sore eyes, Honey! You remind me of my big sister."

Polly spoke before she could bite her tongue, "I'm sure she's very proud of you."

"Shut yer pie hole, or I'll shut it for ya!"

Keep your head about you, Polly. Be quiet!

Then he looked to Martha, the distraught, golden-haired girl still puddled and bawling from where she'd landed. His glare settled on her.

"Well, well, well, hmm, hmm, hmmm! Look what we have us here, boys? Two good lookin' ladies and one just a fresh, tender girl, a real pretty little girl. This job comes with a bonus! We are gonna have us a time around the campfire tonight! I'll go first and then ya'll can draw straws for who goes second.

"Lil' Sweetheart, quit you're damn cryin' and climb on down outta there. Darlin', I want to get a better look at you. Maybe I won't be able to wait 'til tonight."

Martha's sobs silenced, and her eyes grew as big as saucers. The man's threats terrified her. She struggled to follow his orders. Polly reached a hand over to help the girl to her feet. She steadied her too as she began her climb out.

"Now, you, lady, get out here! I'll be damned if you're not a bad lookin' dolly. I might be taking you on after the boss gets done. You know what I'm sayin', don't you?"

Polly was standing now, but not taking the bait. He'd get his eyes scratched out if he tried. She was comforted by the weight of her loaded revolver tucked within the pleats of her heavy skirt. She wouldn't hesitate to kill him if the chance opened up. In fact, she was looking forward to it.

She acted all nervous and petrified as she crawled her

way out of the ruined Concord. She pushed Martha over, so she had ample room to stand by her. It gave Polly a little more room to maneuver if she got to make a play. From this new perspective, Polly counted three outlaws with guns drawn.

A fourth outlaw had been sent around the front of the stage to check on Kriss and retrieve the locked bag from under the seat. All of these men looked like spooks with their faces covered and eyeholes cut out. The effect was ghastly.

"Driver ain't ded yet but will be soon enough. This here's a right heavy bag. For sure, it ain't no letters to Granny." The fourth bandit laughed at his own joke.

"You, man, Humpty Dumpty, in the brown suit, trying to hide back there, are you? Out! My, my, ya all dressed up for a wedding or somethin'? I wanna to see what's in the bag you're carrying."

The rotund man stumbled forward holding his leather satchel under one arm as if he could keep it safe. Polly had turned slightly in order to watch the nervous gentleman. Impressively, he quickly whipped out a two-shot derringer attached to his gold watch fob. Unfortunately, he couldn't hit the broad side of a barn. His two shots went wild. She saw both flashes of the small rounds being wasted.

However, it afforded her the one chance she'd been anticipating. Her body slumped to the ground as if she'd been hit. She landed with her back almost touching the coach, and her right arm appeared to be pinned beneath her body. Her other arm had conveniently come to rest beside her face.

In the following hullabaloo, she managed to keep her eyes hidden but in fact could see through a squint. The dead drummer's blood on the front of her clothes helped complete the illusion she was fatally injured.

Behind her, the creepy little man with the leather bag fell out the door, face first, courtesy of the outlaw who delivered a chest shot from his six-gun. It was a stroke of luck he didn't pin her down, and his bulk actually provided Polly with a little more cover to make a move.

After the gambler and the farmer stepped to the ground and joined the lone cowboy brother, one of the outlaws walked forward and retrieved the dead man's leather bag. Shooting the padlock open, he let out a loud yeehaw when he saw the contents. He held up a sampling of the gold coins and paper money. He handed each of his three compadres a couple of gold pieces to whet their greedy appetites.

"Wull, I'll be a jackass! Check out the mail bags, boys! Let's wrap this up," ordered the man in the lead.

In the three US mailbags taken from the coach's boot, they found nothing greater than personal letters, papers, and such. They threw the contents of all three bags up into the air. The letters were caught and launched into the current of the wind. It looked a little like it was snowing. Evidently, the bag from under the driver's seat held the most lucrative cache they were really after. Without opening it, one of the men looped its handle over his saddle horn.

Two of the outlaws took off on their horses getting away with the take. The thief who'd come out from the front of the stage and the man who'd done the talking stayed behind.

He yelled, "I'll grab the girl, she'll ride with me. We'll kill the others and look through their pockets. Don't leave anyone behind to talk. Too bad about the woman, we were gonna take her with us. Kill them all!"

The farmer charged toward the man told to kill them. In short order he was immediately shot down with a bullet to his head. Polly used his heroic sacrifice to roll fast and come up with the revolver in her hand, aimed confidently. Wasting no time, she struck, and hit her targets. She did it with a bullet left to spare. Her move was totally unexpected by the two outlaws.

She put a neat slug right between the eyes of the man who'd given the orders to kill, and she shot the other one in the neck. She'd gotten lucky and hit a main artery, because he dropped, bleeding out on the ground in a matter of seconds.

You dirty cowards got what was coming to you! I'd do it again if I could!

Polly took two bullets out of her pocket to replace the spent cartridges. She'd been taught to always reload a gun after firing. She returned it to the deep pocket.

The gambler with the white ruffled shirt sat down on the ground shaking his head in his hands, confessing, "I had a derringer up my sleeve but couldn't get to it, no, the truth is I choked."

Stan, the one cowboy left, looked at Polly in admiration.

"Tarnation, Ma'am, I sure thought we were gonners! Where'd ya learn to shoot? I'm mighty thankful you did.

"Ma'am, you saved our lives! I sure wish Cecil had lived to see you shoot. I'd never have believed it myself if I hadn't seen it."

CHAPTER 12

─•◆❖◆•─

THE AFTERMATH

Marshal JD and Ranger Grey Byrd stood with their backs leaning up against the bar with boots crossed at the ankles. They threw back a small glass filled with Red Eye. The amber liquid burned good and hot all the way down.

The Shot 'a Whiskey Saloon was the favorite two-bit watering hole in town. The lawmen had earned the right to wash down all the dust they'd eaten today with a little whiskey. They'd ridden from homestead to homestead questioning farmers and talking to store owners in the small settlements about the rash of robberies.

Recently, men riding on the wrong side of the law were wreaking havoc in Marshal JD's territory, and it had to stop. The mayhem and robberies were in and around Cap Rock, Spur, and Dickens, the county seat, as well as vulnerable isolated farmsteads.

The jobs had elements of being organized and leaning toward the savvy of a seasoned ringleader. JD had been working the cases alone, but he'd called in Ranger Grey Byrd a few days ago for his help.

At first the outlaws only hit soft targets pulling nickel and dime robberies and stealing a few horses. The marshal had hoped the thieves would move out to other territories, but recently the number of reports near here was escalating instead. When citizens started reporting guns being waved around and being threatened bodily, it was a game changer. This gang had to be reined in before someone got killed.

The two friends, JD and Grey, reviewed stacks of wanted posters last night setting aside the ones out-of-date and making a stack of men who'd been spotted by citizens or other lawmakers. Of course, it was possible these outlaws didn't have papers on their heads yet, but it was definitely worth taking a look at the posters. When a wanted poster with a picture of Alex Johns surfaced, Grey picked it up to study more closely. The scar on his cheek made him look tough. He probably got it in a knife fight.

"Wait," Grey asked, "isn't Johns still in a New Mexico prison?"

"He served his time and was released a few months ago."

"Did you ever notice how much the two of you favor? Except for this scar, the resemblance is uncanny."

JD made a disgruntled sound. "Of course, I'm aware of it, but the coincidence is just a coincidence. I know who my parents were, and where I came from in Texas. There's no connection."

"Of course not, sorry I mentioned it."

The lawmen worked putting together a list of bits and pieces of information, details, and descriptions from what little victims could tell them. No matter how vague it was, the two lawmen categorized it in the list. It didn't amount to much as a whole so far.

The biggest strength, and ironically, the biggest weakness in the investigation was the fact no one had seen their faces. It was always the same though, the outlaws carefully covered their features using cloth or bandanas with eyeholes cut out to hide their identities. Sooner or later, this particular habit might give JD and Grey a lead. It wasn't much, but at least it was something.

The profile of the jobs was evolving into higher stakes. People were understandably nervous and alarmed. Many no longer felt safe. So far, no one has been hurt seriously, only properties have been taken. The outlaws had to be stopped and jailed soon before the crime spree turned lethal.

Today's miles in the saddles had produced little fruit for JD and Grey. Even with both of them interrogating witnesses and covering more ground, little new evidence surfaced. The victims had no enlightening clues. No one had seen a face, recognized a voice, heard a name, or could relate any other definitive facts. Except, one farmer had measured a couple of boot prints.

Luckily, no banks had been hit yet, but stores were being broken into under the cover of darkness. They were only discovered the next morning with busted doors or windows and missing merchandise.

The marshal had made a map and marked the locations of hits as they were reported. The number of men involved varied from job to job. In some cases, witnesses were able to determine which way the thieves rode out, but the tracks had disappeared so couldn't be followed.

JD and Grey were regrouping and planned to ride out again early in the morning for another go at it. Someone had to know something but for right now it was a lot of waiting for the next axe to fall.

The two friends were kicking back in the shade for the rest of this day, when a deputy, who'd heard they were back in town, rushed in, flapping the squeaky batwing doors.

"Marshal, a telegram came in asking us to be on the lookout for a lone bank robber. A bank in Abilene was robbed by an inside employee who has disappeared. He took at least $3000 in some cash but mostly gold coins. There's a description and a name. This older gentleman is short, stocky, bald, immaculately dressed, and well-groomed. His name is Edgar Evans, but he's most likely using an alias.

"Oh, and the afternoon stage from Abilene ain't here yet."

This news got their attention! They knocked back what was left in a second round and skipped on thirds offered by the bartender.

It wasn't too uncommon for a stage to be late, but with trouble stirring in the territory, the two men immediately reacted. The deputy was sent for a wagon to transport people and baggage back if necessary. JD sent someone to tell his wife not to expect him until late. JD and Grey hurried to the livery to gather their horses and gear, knowing the deputy would follow as soon as he could get things organized. They needed the wagon in case the stage had broken down.

"JD," said Grey, "I've been hit in the gut with an old familiar feeling churning in the pit of my stomach. It's taught me to prepare to face the worst but pray for the best."

"JD, this doesn't feel right today."

"Grey, I know what ya mean, I feel a dread too, wish we'd had time to eat before we left. It may be a while before we can get back. We'll probably be eatin' hardtack and jerky from our saddlebags before this night's over."

For West Texas lawmen, peace and quiet never lasted long enough. JD had been looking forward to a tasty supper at a café with his longtime friend. He'd planned on his own bed and snuggling up with Lilac tonight. The jailhouse had a room above the office where JD slept before he married. Whenever Grey stayed overnight in Spur, it was his. It looked like these pleasantries might not be in the cards.

They'd ridden out far enough to leave the town behind.

"Well, I'll be damned!" JD spit on the ground and stood up in the stirrups for a better look. "A rider comin' in fast, can't be bringing us anything but trouble, I expect. Shit!"

As soon as the rider was spotted clipping fast from the south, Grey's appaloosa, Spanish Flight, and JD's black gelding, Newman, answered their masters' needs and demands. The two horses picked up their paces in response to slight redistributions of the riders' weights. Going from an easy lope into a gallop was little effort for the powerful and seasoned horses.

Getting closer, JD recognized the older boy from the relay station. Even from this distance, he could see the quarter horse he rode was lathered. The boy had been pushing, so he was on an urgent errand.

His pa must have sent him to town to find JD and report a problem. The Overland Stage was scheduled to stop at the relay station to switch the tired team out for fresh horses before making the last leg into Spur.

As soon as he was close enough, JD cupped his hands around his mouth and hollered to be heard. "What's wrong, what's happened?"

Before pulling up his black as he got closer, he asked, "Where's the stage, Thad?"

Thad was sweating and out of breath from riding hard with important news to deliver. Galloping for an extended period of time is a workout for the rider as well as his horse. His pa had put him on a marbled mare capable of making the run into town.

Thad started the story, rushing out his words interrupted by gulping breaths.

"The stage, Marshal, it never made it to the way station. A cowboy told pa it was a massacre!"

"What cowboy, Son?"

"A cowboy named Stan. He rode into the relay station as fast as he could on one of the holdup men's horses! He and his brother were ridin' on top. His brother took a bullet.

This cowboy came ridin' in and yellin' about what happened. He was grieved over losin' his brother, Cecil, in the fight. Others are dead too!

"Thad, how many were killed?"

"Don't know, but the stage was carrying gold coins. I didn't hear how many died. He needed to get back and help the ladies.

"The woman in charge sent him to the station on an outlaw's horse to get help. He said she was handling the situation."

"You say a woman took charge? Who?"

"Didn't hear the name, Sir."

"We had a feeling, Thad, just had a feeling something was wrong when the stage was late getting in. You did good, Thad, you're a good man. You did your pa proud today."

"Thanks, Marshal!"

"Walk yer mare and cool her down. A deputy'll be coming this way before long, drivin' a cleanup wagon. Tie her on back 'n' hitch a ride to the station."

"Yes, Sir."

CHAPTER 13

REALITY

~*Grey*

The station master's wife and younger boy met them in the relay station yard. She hadn't talked to the cowboy who rode in from the stage herself, but Bob, her husband, said people were seriously hurt, not just passengers. The cowboy was in a hurry to get back and help. Bob fixed him up with a fresh mount, and he took off in a cloud of dust hell bent on returning.

"Bob sent Thad to Spur. We threw food, water, and medical supplies into the buckboard, and he took off in the same direction as the cowboy."

"We're gonna take a quick look at the outlaw's horse and tack, want to see it all, might tell us something," Grey said.

"Horse is here, but not the other. The cowboy put all the tack on the fresh mount. I'll be quick and make you two some biscuit sandwiches to eat on the way out. I bet you haven't had supper."

"No, Ma'am, much obliged," Grey said, putting a finger to the brim of his Stetson. "We'll be leaving just as soon as we have our look. Oh, and your son is headed back this way with a deputy."

The horse was a sorrel carrying the brand and the description of a stolen horse reported last week. It linked the animal to the thieves they were hunting. This was the first big break they'd had in the case.

"Well, Grey, your old feeling was right on the mark. At least we've found out a few things but not enough to know what we're fixin' to ride into. Lord 'a mercy, don't seem like there's ever a lull in mankind's sufferings or meanness.

"We know one cowboy and a lady are still alive. Keep prayin' there are more. The stage from Abilene is usually full. I sure want to talk to this woman who can boss men around. 'M'agine a lady steppin' up to take the reins instead of fanning her face and relying on a man to take care of her."

"Let's get to the sight and have a look at the saddle and saddlebags from the outlaw's horse," Grey said.

"You know Coley's wife, Qynne, is the kind to speak up and take charge of any situation or anyone, man, or woman. She's something else!

"JD, did you know gold was comin' in on the stage today?"

"Naah, must have been a last-minute deal, such has happened before, but usually if it's a big amount I get a telegram. I would have ridden out to meet the stage, Grey, if I'd known. We'll get some answers soon."

Grey didn't say much more on the way to the stage. He pushed Spanish Flight to make better time. At this point, nothing was to be gained by speculation. Until he could evaluate the depth of the disaster himself and question survivors, he didn't have the facts, only hearsay.

Grave silence met them at the sight of the holdup. A few

men were milling around, but no talk was carried in the air. He could see Bob from the relay station and the cowboy who must be, Stan, working with the last two horses in the background. Only the labored breathing of horses could be heard faintly. Four had already been put down. Their carcasses were scattered, and no doubt the last two of the team couldn't be saved either.

The driver had been forced to run them too hard for too long. The horses were left wind broke because they couldn't get enough breath while running and their lungs partially collapsed. A wind broke horse might be able to get air into his lungs but not to be able to get it out except by using abdominal muscles. It caused labored sounds similar to heaving or wheezing. A suffering windblown horse was better off dead in most cases.

Grey had witnessed a lot of tragedies in his years riding with the rangers, and he recognized the signs of a war. Whatever took place here this afternoon was bad, really bad. It looked like a massacre with six bodies laid out under the scant shade of a small tree.

A woman with a thick braid trailing down her back was under the only other tree with a young girl sitting behind her. The lady was bent over an injured man tying off the ends of fresh white bandages she'd wound around his chest. Grey could see signs of blood seeping through the cloth strips. As he'd ridden closer, he recognized the injured man was his friend, Kriss.

No one acknowledged their arrival as Grey ground-tied his appaloosa. The woman's attention was focused solely on Kriss. Now he could see the front of her clothing was smeared and stained red with dried blood.

A young, blonde-headed girl without any hint of expression on her face was slowly rolling strips of cloth into balls to be used for bandages. She lifted her head slightly at the sound of JD and Grey walking up beside her. She spared only a glance at their feet and continued her work.

Two large caliber bullets were lying on a flat stone by the small fire where water was heating in a can. A slender, bloody knife lay by the lead along with a silver flask, a jar of salve, and a bottle of laudanum.

Kriss was restlessly laying on his back, groaning off and on with his eyes closed. The woman offered him kind words and a comforting hand constantly. Grey cleared his throat and asked, "Is he gonna make it."

"Hard to tell yet," she answered wearily, not looking up.

Grey moved on to the row of dead bodies laid out and covered, leaving JD behind to sort this woman's story out.

~Polly Stearns

JD asked gently, "Ma'am, are you alright? Is there anything I can do for you?"

Still, without looking up to identify who was talking to her, she didn't answer his question but told him about the blood on her dress and how it got there.

"The blood on my dress came from the first man murdered. I believe he might have been a drummer. He has an ordering pad and two lead pencils sticking out of his pocket. He wore a bowler hat. I can't even tell you who he was," she swallowed a sob.

"And this man is the driver. Kriss is his name. I didn't like him at first, and he didn't like me either, I think. We mixed about as well as oil and water. I thought he was too gruff and bossy, but now I realize he was just doing a hard job and trying to help us to make the trip safely. Our welfare was the reason he took two bullets. He was doing what he had to do to keep us alive. He's a good man, this one. He's hurt badly, and I'm doing everything I know how to keep him breathing."

She finally looked up to see who was asking her questions. She didn't need the badge pinned to his shirt to know this was her son. Without a word, she stared at him and couldn't stop staring. She was looking into the face of Marshal JD Stearns as he towered above her, large and muscular.

The resemblance between her recollection of Alex Johns and her son was unmistakable. Why should she be surprised a boy would grow to look so much like his father. She'd not prepared to face him today.

There was a lull in her narrative as she looked far away at nothing.

Memories of Alex suddenly flooded her thoughts, taking her away for a moment. Their brief time together flashed through her mind in a second. Alex had been twenty-four and in his prime. The silver-tongued rogue could have sweet talked a baby out of a candy stick. It was exactly what she'd been twenty-seven years ago, a helpless baby with candy.

At fourteen, she didn't understand the ways of a con man, or any man. He'd easily lured her and got whatever he wanted with sweet words flowing from his mouth like honey. Then, Polly was ignorant of life and too innocent to recognize what he wanted from her. Lying with him in the loft had cost her dearly.

Like the unhappy child she was, she'd thought she was head over heels in love and gave him everything she had of worth. She trusted a thieving, lying outlaw who had no conscience.

God, forgive me, please.

"Ma'am, Ma'am you look quite beat, are you sure you're not hurt anywhere? I have questions to ask you while things are fresh on your mind."

"I understand, Marshal. You have your job to do. I'm alright, just quite shaken."

"I can understand, Ma'am, you've been through an ordeal here.

"First, tell me how bad Kriss is? The slugs you took out

and put here on the rock are large caliber."

He slipped them into his shirt pocket for evidence.

"I can see the wounds are still oozing blood."

"One of them went deep into his chest. I had to really dig for it. He's not good, but I think he has a chance if he doesn't get an infection and start fevering. Stan built the fire. I got the slugs out with my knife and cleaned the wounds thoroughly with whiskey from the flask I carry. I stitched them with a needle and embroidery thread I pulled from my satchel.

"The nice man from the relay station brought salve, laudanum, clean water, and some food. I'm heating beef jerky in water for broth. Maybe I can get a little of it down him when he rouses. I'll keep the bandages changed. He can't be moved yet. I'll sit here with him all night."

"You must be bone tired and wrenched, Ma'am, from the ordeal. You've had a bad day."

She softly said, "I've had a lot of terribly bad days before this one, and I've gotten stronger from each one of them. I'll get by and come out the other end. I always do."

CHAPTER 14

————— ◆‑◈‑◆ —————

ANSWERS TO QUESTIONS

"Ma'am, I'll have someone stay here with you and Kriss through the night. What's your name, Ma'am?"

"Melody Potter."

"Where'd ya learn doctorin', Ms. Potter'? Looks like you've done a little of it. Kriss is mighty lucky you knew how to help him."

"Any interactions I've had with Kris have been contentious until now. I'm sure he'll be surprised and ill-tempered to wake up and find me sitting here tending him.

"A lifetime ago I lived with a doctor and his wife in San Antonio. I worked in his office, watched him treat people, assisted him, read his medical books, and I learned. I've seen a lot of bullet wounds, broken bones, amputations, and gruesome injuries from accidents.

"Eventually, when the doctor was out on a call, he trusted me to do what needed to be done. I once dug a slug out while under gunpoint. Can you believe it? It's why I learned how to shoot and carry a gun."

JD caught himself studying this curious female more closely and realized there was a little something familiar about her, but he couldn't put his finger on it. He shook his head and dismissed the thought as nothing. If it was anything important, it would eventually come to him. Judging by her clothing, notwithstanding the blood and dirt, she was dressed like a fine lady.

He could hear the fatigue in her voice and sat down on the ground, so she needn't tilt her head back to talk to him.

"I know you have to be exhausted Ms. Potter, but can you please tell me what happened here?"

"Mmmmm, what happened here, where to start?"

"Start wherever ya, like, Ma'am. I'll tell ya if I need clarification or get lost."

"I was road weary after the trains and riding the stage. I was hot, so, so hot. The wind burned my skin like heat off a stove. There were eight passengers. Six of us rode inside with two cowboys riding topside. They were brothers, Cecil, the older, and Stan.

"Kriss drove the team and Charlie rode shotgun. They were all out in the open together. Charlie and Cecil were killed early in the exchange of fire. Kriss was shot later during the robbery because he stood up to them.

"When poor Charlie Shotgun took a bullet, he fell. I heard and felt the back wheel of the coach run over him. I'll never be able to forget the sound or the sickening bump of the wheels going over his body. The memory makes me feel sick to my stomach."

Polly stopped talking and put her hand to her mouth. JD handed her his bandana and she just sat still for a long moment. She finally looked at him, but more than just a look, she stared at him. Finally, she broke her silence and began to talk again.

"He's lying over there, you know, Charlie, stone cold with the others, hard to think about such a nice young man losing his life to senseless madness.

"Why can't the evil in the world be content only to go after the evil and leave good people alone?

"I had the two passengers left to layout the bodies in a row under what little shade there is. I wanted the bodies organized so the best of the men could rest in peace. The outlaws don't deserve such respect. They lived by the sword and died by the sword.

"I had them rip down the canvases from the windows and use them to cover the men. I said to leave their pockets and saddle bags alone for the law to go through their belongings, except for Cecil, of course. Cecil's things belong to Stan. I knew you'd be coming. I've heard about you, Marshal."

Again, JD stared at her and shook his head.

"Thank you, Ms. Potter. Ranger Byrd's goin' through all of it now. We'll be talkin' to the other passengers, including the girl here.

"No, Martha is mine. She is my traveling companion. You can't talk to her yet because she's still in shock. She's nearly scared out of her wits. Let's not demand she say anything yet. She'll come around when she feels safe and settled. Then you can talk to her."

"Okay, I agree, Ma'am, I won't bother her until she's ready."

Polly digressed back to the beginning, "The trail narrowed considerably all of a sudden, and Kriss slowed the team down. On one side of us was the tall sea of grass and on the other was the treacherously jagged canyon edge."

"Yah, I know the place."

"All of a sudden, he started popping the whip, shouting, and putting the horses into a reckless run as fast as they could go. The mood changed. At the time, I couldn't figure out why, well, I suspected the reason but couldn't face it. One of the back wheels slipped over the sharp edge.

"I assumed we'd go over the side, but Kriss kept urging the horses to run faster and faster trying to get the Concord onto solid footing again. The noise was loud and grinding! When the coach finally took purchase, I could feel the unstableness of the wheel. It wobbled but miraculously kept turning.

"Once started, the gunfire didn't let up, and I had to admit to myself we'd been ambushed. I heard the shots coming from behind us and the return shots answered from up top. A bullet penetrated the back of the coach, splintering wood. It hit one of the passengers."

She paused, and when she spoke again, her words were almost whispered.

"Hit the back of his head, and the bullet came out his forehead, killed him instantly, the poor man fell forward, face down into my lap, I panicked and pushed him as hard as I could to the floor. I shouldn't have been so disrespectful and uncaring, but I was terrified and just reacted with revulsion. Back and forth bullets kept reporting and answering for I don't know how long.

I can't recall when we all scrambled to the floor joining the lifeless man. We didn't talk about it or make a unanimous decision. It seemed like we just dove at the same time as a unit. A horse screamed, and the coach shuddered and rattled before it came to a complete stop. I realized the wheel had finally splintered. We were leaning at a tilt on the back axel on account of it."

Polly's voice wound down.

JD took the time to look around him while she checked on Kriss. The Overland Stage was sitting cockeyed off a piece at the angle she'd described. The relay man and cowboy were walking the two horses without signs of improvement. They'd tried their best, but JD still heard the labored breathing from where he was sitting.

There was hardly a chance a horse with damaged lungs would ever be useful for anything again. The men were struggling to keep them from lying down to die. Injured horses had little willpower to live. Two shots pierced the silence and JD and the woman both flinched. The last of the horses had been put down.

Envelopes and papers were scattered near and far. Some were hung up against scrubby bushes, stuck on thorns, in clumps of cactus, and wedged between blades of the tall grass. Pieces of mail were spread out in the distance. A man in a ruffled shirt was gathering the papers and stuffing them back into mailbags. No doubt some of the letters were already long gone forever. They'd been posted in the West Texas wind for only the rattlesnakes to read.

"Ms. Potter could ya commence the tellin' of your story again. The way you tell it, I can almost see what happened as clear as day. You're being most helpful. Start from where you left off when the coach was dragged to a stop."

"I could hear horses galloping closer, and there were whistles like the riders had signals. I couldn't hear any voices, but I knew exactly when the horses stopped outside the coach, I knew when whoever had chased us put feet on the ground. The door was ripped open with so much force it banged, hitting the side of the Concord.

"What I saw shocked me, Marshal. The man blocking the doorway was wearing a red bandana, stretched out in a diamond-shape. It covered his entire face with a corner hanging below his chin. The top corner was under his hat. It must have been tied behind his head because it was securely in place. Eyeholes had been cut out so he could see. It was a startling sight. He was more spook than man!

"It's odd what crazy things a person will think when frightened.

"I could see when his attention stopped on Martha, and he held his eyes on her. Then his glare came to settle on me. I'll be looking into the monster's eyes in my sleep for a while."

"What color were his eyes?"

"Brown shades like the dry grass, every color of the prairie. Though knowing won't do you a bit of good. He's dead." Her eyes traveled to the line of dead men.

JD followed her line of vision to where Grey had stood not long ago.

"Who shot him?"

Polly ignored his question but continued recounting her story.

"The spook looked back at Martha making her cry all the harder. He cursed, ordering her to shut up, stop the racket. She did her best and quieted down, choking. I don't fault her for crying. She's a child. I thought about it a time or two myself, but anger won out over tears."

"I asked you who shot him. I need to know who killed him."

She sighed deeply and continued.

"Two of the outlaws took the money bags and rode out fast. Then the man who'd been giving the orders said the girl would ride with him to be passed around. Before he grabbed her, he ordered the man who stayed behind to kill the rest.

He said, "Don't leave even one alive!"

"I was lying on the ground playing dead already. Right after he said this, I rolled and took my chance. I shot them both before they had time to react. I shot both of them, one in the head and the other in the neck. I think they never knew what hit them. I killed both of them, Marshal, before they could kill us!"

JD knit his eyebrows together. It was time to take a break.

"We'll finish this later, Ms. Potter. I want to talk to you some more, but right now, you need to try and sleep a while before Kriss rustles again. He'll be needing you."

~JD

He was stunned by what the woman said. The outlaws had misjudged Melody Potter, and so had JD.

Seven corpses lying still and neatly in a row were separated from the living by distance, circumstances, and reality. It saddened JD to see Charlie Shotgun, laid out among them. His name was really Charlie Sagar, but everyone called him Charlie Shotgun because of his job.

What a waste! JD knew he was a husband, a father, and an all-around good guy. Lilac and his wife, Sallie, were good friends. Their families shared picnics.

He'd ridden out in the open with Kriss for the last three years just working to make a living for his young family. Poor Charlie never had a chance on this run. From the looks of his body, he'd been shot in the chest and run over by the heavy Concord after he'd fallen. It was like Ms. Potter thought. He couldn't help but wonder if Kriss would wind up in this line with him.

Another man was dressed in dark, dusty clothing like a preacher might wear, and a bowler hat sat in his grey hands lying on his chest. Ms. Potter thought he must be a peddler who accidently was shot in the head. There was a young cowboy with no bandana, who must be Cecil, Stan's brother. They were riding up top together. His luck ran plumb out today.

The next passenger had to be Edgar Evans. He fit the description in the telegram he'd gotten this afternoon from Abilene. He'd send a telegram back to the sheriff there to call off the manhunt. This man was short, paunchy, balding, and dressed like a dude in shiny shoes and expensive clothes. He didn't make it very far with the money he'd stolen.

Grey already removed the ridiculous masks from the two outlaws' faces. Whatever he'd found in their pockets was laid out on their chests along with the disguises which also linked them to the recent robberies.

This was the second break in the case, so there was no

doubt they were hot on the heels of the bandits. The third and most important break would be the bullets once he had them all. They could be traced back to the guns used to fire them.

He'd have to recover Ms. Potter's bullets from the outlaws.

JD had noticed Grey talking to the gambler, who was gathering mail. Only the cowboy was left to interrogate.

He and Grey would have some interesting notes to compare later.

CHAPTER 15

ED SCHMIDT, CRAZY OUTLAW

Polly slept for three days when she reached Mabel's Boarding House before she ventured out again. Today she had planned to slip quietly into the Shot 'a Whiskey Saloon without causing a scene, but the damn, squeaky butterfly door hinges announced her entrance like a town fire bell. They flipped and flapped noisily back and forth as she cleared the threshold. The backlighting of the bright morning sun made her feminine form be seen as a dark silhouette.

The random range of voices, laughter, jingling spurs, and even pool balls hitting on impact seemed to stop in unison. It went stone cold silent as if a spigot had been turned. The sudden silence was louder than the chaos.

It was too early for the place to be packed to capacity. The patrons there had turned in chairs or lifted heads from conversations and card games. They were curious about whom had entered the bar. Stepping deeper into the smoke-ladened room prolonged the pronounced hush her arrival caused. It wasn't every day a real lady came into a place like this for a drink.

The unabashed curiosity of the rough looking men prompted her to reconsider the mission she'd set out to accomplish. No one could possibly suspect who she was. She felt confident, her identity was unknown.

She was undaunted by the staring eyes and moved full steam ahead to the polished bar on her right with no hesitation in her steps whatsoever. Being accountable for Martha's safety made this visit necessary.

Harpy, the owner, was working behind the bar. He schooled his surprise as if women of her caliber were regular patrons. She found it rather amusing, the bartender never stopped drying a large tray of clean glasses and showed her no interest until she was belly-up to the counter.

"What can I do for ya today, Ma'am?" he asked. "Mostly we serve beer, whiskey, and not much for the ladies, unless yer needin' a drink a water."

She leaned closer ignoring his limited list of offerings. She softly answered the man with an inquiry of her own, "By any chance is the marshal here?"

Her low voice let Harpy know this lady didn't want anyone else to hear her business. He took the hint and answered-in-kind.

"Naah, deputies neither, don't come in 'til later in the day usually unless there's trouble. Check his office why don't cha?"

Continuing to whisper, she said, "I went there first. Can you tell me if you know a man by the name of Ed Schmidt?"

"Eddie? Yeah, I know him, everybody does, but Ma'am I gotta tell ya he's no account. Whatda ya want to see him for? Whatever it is, cancel yer plans pronto is my free advice, lady."

"Thanks for the warning. I'm sure it's made from sage

insight. Where can I find him?"

Looking over Polly's shoulder, he nodded once in the direction behind her. "He's sittin' over there against the back wall, but you hear me good Lady, don't approach him. Word has it he's knee deep into somethin', and Marshal JD's got eyes on 'im."

Without heeding his words, she turned and looked Ed Schmidt right in the face. His black hair was bushy and unkept, and his eyes appeared dark. There was a brief moment she recognized those glassy eyes but dismissed the notion. The handlebar mustache he sported was absurdly big for his small, rat-like pointed nose. Their eyes locked, and a chill coursed through her. She was shaken but remained cool. Maybe coming here was a mistake.

Turning back to the bar, she asked, "Where is his farm located?"

"His farm?" Harpy laughed. "There's a man who's never done an honest day's work in his life. He don't own no farm er much else except a horse and a gun, and he prob'ly stole the horse.

"It ain't none of my business why a nice lady like you would want to find his worthless hide, but take my advice, walk outta here, and fergit it!"

"Mmmm, I don't doubt you're telling me the truth. Thank you for the information. I'll keep trying to catch up with the marshal."

"If he comes in, what do ya want me to tell him for ya?"

"Tell him Melody Potter wants to talk to him. It's urgent. He'll know my name. I'll be at Mabel's Boarding House."

Polly and Martha shared a room at the boarding house. They ate their meals in the kitchen together. Polly didn't want Martha to be seen any more than necessary. Martha hadn't been outside all week since the stage holdup. Polly saw signs she was greatly improving but still affected by the worst scare of her life.

She was also homesick, but Polly couldn't figure out why she'd miss her people who'd kicked her out the door. It would be a great mistake for her to go back to Abilene. Polly could well sympathize with the separation anxiety the young girl was feeling, but she'd get over it. Hadn't she, herself, been forced out of a terrible home long ago? It was the only home and way of life she'd ever known.

Polly had possession of the hateful note Ed Schmidt had mailed to Martha when he sent money for her stage passage. The more times she read it; the more the woman believed this man was capable of hurting Martha.

Over Polly's dead body would he ever get his hands on Martha. It was a possibility he would meet every stage coming into Spur looking for his mail order victim. Martha wouldn't survive a man like Polly had seen today in the saloon.

Polly was willing to do whatever it took to keep him away from her. She'd listened to Harpy's words this morning and had taken them seriously. One look at the guy with his chair precariously leaning back against the wall, and she'd felt cold go through her body. Polly was convinced Martha Wheatley needed more protection than she alone could provide.

There was a knock at the door. Polly assumed it was one of Mabel's hired girls coming to visit Martha. They were about the same age, and her daily visits had lightened her ward's spirit. The girl was good company. This time, however, she had a message for Polly.

"Ms. Potter, the marshal is downstairs waiting to see you. I'll sit with Martha a while."

"Oh, I'm sure she'll enjoy your company. I'm so glad you two have become friends. I'll be back directly." Both girls smiled, already starting to jabber with each other. This was the best medicine Martha could possibly have. Polly loved the chance to see her son again, though he was none the wiser who she was. She couldn't reveal their intertwined story just yet. She had to confide in Lilac first. She was the grease Polly hoped to use to smooth the shock. Seeing him waiting for her at the parlor table with a small, pink porcelain cup of coffee in his hand made her heart race momentarily. He couldn't even get his thick fingers into the space the handle afforded. Her son was a big, muscled man and the table looked ridiculously out of proportion with his size.

"Marshal, thank you for coming right away. There's something pressing you need to know about Martha Wheatley. I fear I cannot keep her safe without your help."

"Harpy said you were looking for me, and he's a might concerned you've already stirred something up. He thinks you're the one who may be in trouble, Ms. Potter. Since words are out around town about how handy you are with a gun and doctoring to boot, you have quite a reputation. People are wondering who you are?

"Begin at the beginning, Ms. Potter? What in the hell is goin' on with you?"

"Marshal, you need to know who Martha Wheatley really is, and why I've taken her under my wing. The first time I saw the girl was when she boarded the stage in Abilene. She was dressed poorly, had no possessions except a small, empty reticule, and it wasn't until later I discovered how starved she was for food and attention. Marshal, I only recognized a small, lost girl in trouble."

"Call me JD, Ma'am."

"Well, alright, of course, JD.

"We weren't actually traveling together as I led you to believe. I'm sorry. The more the girl and I were together on the arduous journey, I surmised she was alone in the world and had been manipulated into a bad situation not of her making. She needed me to claim her.

"I tried to stay disengaged from her situation because I had my own problems worrying me. Then I realized the extent of Martha's trouble. Once the stage got held up, I knew the child needed me to protect her for sure.

"After what I learned this morning, I'm afraid she and I may both need help. I'm unsure of how to proceed.

"Martha Wheatley is fourteen years old. The girl was forced on this trip to Spur by herself, because of a negligent mother. She boarded the Overland Stage in Abilene at the same time I did. I didn't really pay much attention to the little mouse at first.

"During the overnight layover, I could tell she was hungry, actually, starving would be a better way to put it. I doubted she had any money to feed herself. I had no intention of eating the swill at the way station, but I had good food and offered to share it.

I befriended her, and we ate in the empty stagecoach. I found out through conversation she was a mail order bride! She was on her way to meet a Mr. Ed Schmidt in Spur to marry and work on his farm. The girl was so young, neglected, and abandoned. It broke my heart!"

JD had sat up a little taller and leaned forward when the name, Ed Schmidt, was spoken by the woman.

"Go on, Ma'am. What else?"

"She's the oldest of seven children, and her ma and pa are dirt poor, cruel parents. After her fourteenth birthday, she was kicked out. Her ma told her it was time she left home and took responsibility for herself.

"She made the girl answer a mail order bride advertisement posted in the paper from a man named Ed Schmidt. He wrote back right away sending the money for passage along with a dire warning written on paper. It's the exact opposite of an inviting love note.

"Here, I have the note in my pocket."

She handed the grimy, wrinkled piece of paper to JD. The marshal frowned as he read the callous warning making it clear if the girl cheated him, he'd make her sorry she ever lived. It was a threat.

"Nothing about this is alright, no doubt about it, he's up to no good and dangerous". I'll keep this if you don't mind."

"Please do!

"I told Martha, she didn't have to marry this crude man or any other man not of her own choosing. I promised she was safe with me. Since the robbery, I've been keeping her out of sight. I thought to do a little investigating on her behalf.

"After this morning, I've become uncertain I'm able to keep her away from harm alone. Since speaking with Harpy and seeing the scoundrel, I'm not even sure how to protect myself anymore."

"You should have come to me first, Ma'am. I'm worried you've stirred up a hornet's nest."

"Harpy said this man doesn't have a farm, a steady job, or much of anything. In fact, he told me he's dangerous, and I'd better stay away from him. I was able to get a good look at the man, though. His appearance made me anxious. I think I know him! Both Martha and I definitely need your help, Marshal."

"What do you mean you think you know him?"

"When our eyes locked together in the saloon, a chill ran through me. His eyes, I recognize his eyes. They made me feel very unsure of myself. I think he might have been one of the men at the stage."

JD frowned, "You ought to be afraid, Ms. Potter, for a fact.

"Eddie Schmidt is a lazy outlaw of sorts. I've had my eye on him for a while. I already have reason to suspect he was one of the men who held up your stage a week ago. You may have just verified it.

"Since you've seen him and thought about it, do you still think he might be one of the robbers?"

"I don't know for sure, but his dark eyes seemed familiar for some reason. The outlaws wore those peculiarly tied bandanas covering their faces. I could only see their eyes, so I couldn't identify any one of them in particular. We looked each other right in the eye, and a bad feeling came over me. If it was him, he could have recognized me this morning.

"Yeah, 'bout this mornin', Ma'am. Harpy said when you turned to get a look at Eddie, he stared directly back at you even after you turned away. There's no way of knowing for sure if he recognized you from somewhere, but Harpy's pretty sure he did.

"After you left the saloon, he came up to the bar asking questions, trying to find out what you wanted. If Harpy's suspicions are correct, you and Miss Martha can't stay here. I've got to get the two of you out of Spur and hidden away until I can get a handle on things.

"Ranger Byrd and I suspect Alex Johns formed a new gang working the territory, and we think Ed's riding with him. I've been on Ed's tail since before the stage hold-up. Harpy has been helping keep an eye on him too."

Alex Johns' gang? No, no, surely, it can't be true.

"I've got to get you and Martha out of town immediately. I'll be picking you up tomorrow before daybreak. Be ready. I'll bring a buckboard around for you and whatever you need to take along. Plan on being gone until this is all settled."

"Where are you taking us?"

"Ranger Grey Byrd's family has a ranch in the next county. His people are plenty nice. You'll like them. You and Martha will be safe there. There are men always around keeping their eyes open.

"Ms. Potter, Ms. Potter, the color's left your face, are you okay?

"You look like you've just seen a ghost.

"Can I get ya some water?"

"A little bit of water isn't going to do me any good, JD. I need a nip or two from my flask.

"Thanks anyway."

CHAPTER 16

MARY ANN SHUMEYER BARTON BYRD

Who am I, really?

This was the one question plaguing Mary Ann since Grey had her pa, BB Barton, declared legally dead in 1880. Mary Ann just wanted to let sleeping dogs lie. Her husband had encouraged her to dig deeper into her past. He didn't understand she was cynical and could live without what she didn't know. She remembered going to the bank in Spur like it was yesterday. It had been a raw and painful experience.

~

BREAK SEAL ONLY UPON the DEATH OF BB BARTON
or by the REQUEST of MARY ANN BARTON

~

Lying dormant for more than three decades in Spur's Texas Bank & Trust vault was an envelope hidden at the very back among the important papers. She hadn't known any such thing with her name on it existed.

It was one of those over-sized legal envelopes sealed with a hardened red wax. The wax had cracked with age. As a precaution, it was also secured with a linen string wrapped tightly around a celluloid circle the size of a shirt button. The written label was a bit cryptic. Mary Ann was apprehensive when she read her name.

"This packet and its contents were deposited in the bank's vault long before I took over my elderly father's position as bank president," Mr. Merkel Tessler said not speaking to Mary but directly but to her husband, Grey Byrd.

The president continued, "Mr. Byrd, the bank has never had the authority to speak of or to break the seal of this packet until now. Even though you're holding Mr. Barton's county death certificate in your hand, I still have to wait for your verbal confirmation before I can unseal it.

"The presence of his daughter, now Mrs. Mary Ann Byrd, certainly meets the criteria of the directives written on the front, but being a married woman, well, you know how the law reads."

Grey squeezed his wife's hand and gave a quick nod to the man.

Merkel graciously extended a pudgy hand inviting them to be seated.

"Please, take your seats, Mr. and Mrs. Byrd, and we'll examine these contents together."

He emptied the envelope on his desktop. There were several papers, and it took several minutes for him to spread, organize, and rearrange them in order to his satisfaction. The pages were yellowed and crisp around the edges since they'd not seen the light of day for so long. The years had taken their toll.

Still not including Grey's wife in the discussion of her own business, he spoke, making eye contact only with her husband.

"Now, this page is the original deed and description of Barton's land. It's made out not to him but to Mrs. Byrd's mother, Alice Shumeyer."

Tapping an index finger on a specific paragraph, he said, "There is a stipulation added in the event Alice Shumeyer is deceased.

"This second page transfers all entitlements to her child when such child reaches legal age. So, clearly this document dates back to before the birth of your wife.

"I seem to recall Ms. Shumeyer passed on years ago of influenza or so BB Barton claimed. It put the town in quite an uproar. BB Barton buried her immediately after death right on this property before he told anyone she was gone. He insisted at the time he was afraid the infectious disease could be spread from her to the folks in town. No one had examined her body, so the man's words were accepted as fact. However, gossips spread rumors like wildfire with suspicions he'd killed her."

"Mr. Tessler, I see you're still wanting to spread the gossip and rumors, yourself, and they're hurtful. Stop being the bearer of old tales. Also, stop referring to my wife, Mrs. Byrd, as if she's not present. Whatever we find out today is her business, her inheritance, do you understand me? You will treat her with the respect she deserves, or you and I aren't gonna get along!"

Tessler's face turned red as a beet. He cleared his throat and answered very quietly. "As you wish, Sir."

Grey turned to look at Mary Ann, "Well, I'll be damned! Mary, you and your mother had ownership rights to BB's farmstead all along. He kept his mouth shut because it was in his best interests to keep this knowledge a secret, the dirty dog!"

Mary made no comment. What was there she could say to dispute the obvious?

"Keep going, Mr. Tessler, Grey ordered. "What else?"

"Based on the next page, BB Barton was not your father at all Mrs. Byrd. Your legal name should have been Mary Ann Shumeyer. Mary Barton, the name you grew up under, is not really who you are."

Mary Ann drew a deep breath and released it slowly. Grey reached for her hand. She and her children were forever a part of the Byrd Ranch Legacy now. She wished for the meeting to be hurried along. Already these papers posed questions without answers.

"The following page speaks of a silent benefactor who provided a home for you and your mother, and a lump sum of cash given directly to BB Barton in exchange for the appearance of marriage.

"I think it's probable the unnamed benefactor may be your actual father or at least someone in his family, Ma'am.

"Oh, sorry, Mr. Byrd, for over-stepping myself again. There is an unnamed benefactor, and that's all I know. I have no knowledge who it might be! My apologies, Mrs. Byrd.

"Here on the bottom of the fifth page, Barton signed a contract agreeing to claim the child Alice carried as his own. In the event BB Barton broke the contract, he would forfeit his home.

"The last page is signed by both Barton and Miss Shumeyer. She promised to maintain silence as well, or the property would be rescinded back to the benefactor."

"Mr. Tessler, clarify this for me, please, are you saying the land where Mary Ann lived and almost starved to death for years was rightfully hers all along? You mean BB Barton's place, the small farm, was never actually his property at all?

"If I heard you right, I'd tear him apart with my bare hands right now if he wasn't already dead!"

"Yes, you are correct."

Withdrawn, Mary Ann sat in the office beside her husband. The president's bushy, caterpillar eyebrows rose above the delicate golden rims of his spectacles. The frames were ridiculously small and delicate for a man of his size. He looked like a clown with them balanced on top of his bulbous nose. Only the sight of this pompous fool wasn't making her laugh.

"Apparently, as I understand the wording Mrs. Byrd, your mother and BB Barton weren't truly married, so she could have claimed the land at any time. But according to Texas law, at present, your husband owns the homestead because a married woman can't own property or keep personal income without her husband's permission.

"Your wife, excuse my bluntness, Mr. Byrd, doesn't actually own this property, you do. You'll need a lawyer and these papers to have the deed transferred over to your name, Mr. Byrd."

"What you just said may very well be the law, but in my house, this land belongs to Mary Ann, and I'll do whatever she decides to do with it. She's certainly earned the right through blood, sweat, and tears. This piece of land has cost her plenty already!"

"Oh, yes, very well, of course. I meant no disrespect."

He cleared his throat before continuing his assessment.

"It seems these disclosures still leave a few unanswered questions for you, don't they? The answers could, more than likely, remain a mystery forever since Alice and BB are both deceased, and the benefactor is not named here."

"Wait! Who's been paying the taxes on this property all these years?" asked Grey. "Surely not BB! JD says Barton never had a dime or a nickel to his name for longer than a day. He spent it on whiskey and gambling."

Merkel called out to a clerk in a small adjoining office asking him to bring the ledger with recorded tax payments and arrears. Opening the book to the correct page, his eyes widened in surprise. "Oh!

"It appears a solicitor, by the name of Orson Wellington, has kept them paid for the client who wishes to remain anonymous. As solicitor, he has always sent the funds directly to the county office. This bank receives a list of payments made to the county, and my clerks record the figures in this ledger.

"However, there may be an address for the solicitor. You might be able to get it from the Dicken's County Seat."

The meeting with the Texas Bank & Trust blind-sided Mary and surprised Grey. She'd heard too much disturbing information piled on top of all the lies and terrible memories from her childhood. On the way back to the ranch, she let Grey know she didn't want to discuss this any further. She did agree to Grey talking to the ranch's lawyer in order to get a clean deed of ownership established in Grey's name.

Mary Ann considered the farmstead to be a closed subject once the new deed was locked away in the ranch's safe. She never considered the taxes due on her land because Grey never failed to pay them.

He offered several times to sell the land and put the money in the bank under her name, but she had no desire to pull the scabs off of old wounds. Mary Ann hadn't even set foot on the property since she'd married Grey. Her mother's grave was there along with the many ghosts of the past.

In time, she did come to terms with her damaged feelings on the matter and wondered if a happy home could ever be built on the land. Mary Ann concluded she wanted the land sold so it might be of use to someone.

She insisted the bill of sale to include an addendum preserving her mother's gravesite. Before putting the property up for sale, Grey preserved the gravesite similar to Frank McGee's resting place on Byrd Ranch.

She was relieved to think her past could rest once and for all. She never imagined her childhood had yet more tricks in store for her!

CHAPTER 17

SECRET OF THE GOLDEN LOCKET

~*Mary Ann Stearns*

Mary Ann remembered the day she married Grey Byrd. It was clearly etched in her mind's eye. She could call the pleasant memory up to revisit at any time and often did. The recollection always started with a handsome stranger standing with JD Stearns on the porch. His friend had come looking for her, a starving, pregnant girl facing winter without a home.

Sheriff JD Stearns had always been kind to her and was always checking on her when she was at her lowest. This time, he brought his friend, Ranger Grey Byrd, to rescue her. He had a serious problem of his own. He stood alongside JD with hat in hand. Both she and the ranger's circumstances had landed them both between two different rocks and two different hard places.

JD had explained her situation to his friend beforehand. The ranger explained his own personal dilemma to her in detail. Both of them were faced with problems neither could solve alone. He proposed an arrangement benefiting them both. For agreeing to mother his sick baby, he promised marriage and agreed to be the father her unborn baby needed.

The answers to their immediate troubles were to work as a team. Their backgrounds were miles apart, but the two babies bonded them together in a united cause. They were determined to join their lives together and make a marriage work.

Sheriff JD Stearns officiated the brief vows, declaring them man and wife. On the day she wed, she became mother to tiny Sari Byrd, and Byrd Ranch became her home.

Her husband, in name only, waited with JD outside while she gathered her belongings. All she owned fit easily into a five-pound flour sack. She tied a faded hand-me-down bonnet under her chin. By faith, she entrusted her future to the ranger and rode away with him on the great, white stallion, Pegasus, to Byrd Ranch.

He'd tied the small sack of her possessions onto the horse's saddle. The treasures had been a Bible and a locket left behind by a mother she hardly remembered. The delicate gold locket held the only image she had of her Ma on one side. On the other, was the likeness of a man who'd never had a name. She only knew he wasn't, BB Barton.

~Grey

After meeting with Merkel Tessler, the bank president, Grey sent a letter of inquiry to Orson Wellington hoping to identify the benefactor of the land. Several months followed with no answer, and he quit expecting a post.

Early one morning near the end of winter, while the cold north wind still blew, and the overcast sky was spitting snow, a buggy rolled into the yard. Thankfully, Grey hadn't ridden out yet and was still in the barn. He came out to greet the visitor. Mary Ann's shut door to the past was blown wide open. In fact, what the man had come to say would set her world into a spin like a child's top.

A well-dressed gentleman extended his hand to Grey. "My name is Oliver Thomas III from Sweetwater. I received word from Orson Wellington about an inquiry he'd received from a Mr. Grey Byrd. I have traced him to this ranch. Tell me, Sir, might you be Grey Byrd?"

"Yes, pull your buggy into the barn, and one of my men will care for your horse. We'll go to my office to talk before my wife knows you're here."

"Of course, Mr. Byrd, I believe it's a most prudent way to proceed. You see, I have quite a story to share, and you'll no doubt want to prepare Mrs. Byrd before she hears it. It's bound to be a jolt, I am sure."

Grey built a fire in his office and asked Maude to bring a tray of biscuits, butter, jam, and coffee. Both men engaged in small talk until the housekeeper set the tray down and left them alone.

"Okay, let's get right to the point of the matter, Mr. Thomas. Tell me what you came to discuss."

"Very well, I'm your wife's half-brother."

Grey blinked and squinted at the stranger. "Whoa, before you continue, I'm going to need some bourbon, I think. Would you care to join me, Oliver, if I may call you Oliver?"

Grey pulled open his bottom desk drawer and retrieved the bottle of fine whiskey and two small glasses. "

"Yes, to both, please, and I will call you Grey. It's not every day a man gets to meet his brother-in-law for the first time."

"You seem mighty sure of this. Maybe, I'll be more inclined to believe your claim after I've heard the whole story. No offense, but I don't know you or how Mary will take such news. You'll have to convince me you're telling the truth.

She had a hard, miserable life before coming to the Byrd Ranch. She grew up barely having enough to eat and sometimes nothing to eat at all. I don't intend to let the past bring her more grief if I can avoid it."

"Completely understandable.

"My father, Oliver Thomas II owned the best saloon in Sweet Water. It was before the name of the town was written as a compound word instead of two separate words. The Kiowa Indians first called it Mobeetie which means sweet water.

"There were five saloons then. Four were small one-bit bars where a cowboy paid one-bit for a glass of cheap, watered-down, liquor and got into fights. Clientele could tap women in the back rooms for a price if you get my meaning.

"The Crystal House, my pa's palace, was the only two-bit saloon in Sweet Water. He sold good whiskey for two-bits a glass giving the buyer back ten cents to buy the second drink. The beer was chilled, and decent food was served. A man could even take his wife in for a good beefsteak on Friday night. There was music and dancing for the couples. Good women worked in the kitchen, on the floor serving, or selling tickets, so single men could dance with a lady.

"Sweet Water had no bank at the time, but Father was well-respected and trusted. Farmers, residents, and merchants deposited their money with him for safe keeping. At one time, he had a vault with more than $20,000 in cash he was holding for citizens and the community. Everyone trusted him.

"Word got out Sweet Water didn't have a real bank, but instead, the owner of The Crystal House kept the town's money locked up for safe keeping. In February of 1862, outlaws considered it to be easy pickings and raided Crystal House. My father was shot and killed defending the money.

Others fought beside him.

"A total of eleven outlaws and citizens were wounded or died in the robbery. The citizens put up a good fight. None of the outlaws got away, and no money was stolen. The very next month, a man named Trammel and a few other business-minded men started the process of establishing the first real bank in Sweet Water."

Grey filled Oliver's glass again.

"Why in the hell are you telling me all this? I can't see it has anything to do with my Mary Ann."

"Bear with me, indeed it does, Grey. Oliver Thomas II was her father as well as mine."

Grimacing, Grey took another sip. "Go on."

"This is where the story my Mother told me on her death bed begins, and it has everything to do with my sister and your wife.

Grey continued filling Oliver's glass every time it was empty. He matched Oliver drop for drop.

Unbeknownst to mother, Father had taken a liking to one of the good women working in his employ. Her name was Alice Shumeyer. He must have really been drawn to her because she became pregnant with his child.

"Being a man of honor, he was forced to face my mother with the torrid affair. As hard as it was for him to speak of this careless infidelity, it was harder yet to convince mother she was the only woman he truly loved. He begged forgiveness for being such a fool as to risk their happy life together.

"She demanded Father prove his love by agreeing to specific demands. Rather quickly, he had to make Alice Shumeyer relocate far away from Sweet Water. In short order, he acquired a homestead near Spur and paid a local to take Alice and the unborn babe off his hands. The man swore to take her as his wife and claim the baby she carried.

"A private solicitor handled the purchase of the land, the

paperwork, all the necessary legal agreements my Father stipulated, and he kept the taxes paid for years."

"You mean your father never checked on his child?"

"No, actually he didn't get a chance, but I believe he would have. Soon after the deal was settled, he died in the attempted robbery at The Crystal House. He never even knew if the baby was a girl or a boy. I was an only child when my father was murdered. Mother kept my only sibling a secret from me until not long before she breathed her last breath.

"I didn't know my sister even existed until a month ago when Mr. Wellington forwarded your letter to me. There was no question in my mind about coming here to meet my sister as soon as I could get away."

Oliver took a picture from his pocket and laid it on the desk in front of Grey.

Grey took one look at it and said, "Hold on, give me a minute."

Grey got up immediately and pulled his wife's golden locket from the ranch's safe. He opened it and said, "Look, it's the same picture. Mary has had a picture of her real father beside her mother all these years. She didn't know who this man was.

"Well, I'll be damned! It's good to finally meet you, Grey!"

CHAPTER 18

WELCOME TO THE RANCH

Polly sent her assistant, Vella, and her foreman, Deets, ahead of her to Spur. They had arrived three months before Polly joined them. Vella and Deets worked together on the necessary groundwork for Polly's mail order bride business.

They'd secured a suitable building to refurbish on Front Street. Deets had just finished a comfortable, private apartment for Vella's living quarters upstairs. Everything was proceeding on schedule as planned.

Vella moved into her new space a few days before Polly arrived in Spur. Everything was fresh, clean, and smelled of new paint. Cheery curtains graced the apartment windows. It was the perfect place for Vella.

Deets had partitioned the downstairs of the building into a reception area, two offices, and a mailroom. A most impressive sign was propped behind the counter ready and waiting to be hung at the right moment announcing The *West to East Matrimonial Agency* was open for business.

Vella had searched for properties to build Polly's house. It would be similar to the boarding house for single women she had in San Antonio but not as large. There weren't many suitable sites available on the edge of town.

By a stroke of luck, Mary Ann Byrd's land became available. This part of Texas was covered by grasslands, rock outcroppings, cacti, sage, and bushy cedars. It had an appealing, rustic, wild look.

Deets drew up the house plans and hired workers from surrounding farms as carpenters. The chance to work in exchange for extra cash to supplement incomes was seen as a Godsend by the locals, and it was a boon to the economy as well. Building materials from area businesses would be used as much as possible. Supplies not easily acquired could be freighted into Spur.

JD's insistent hurry to relocate Martha and herself made sense, and her work here was well in hand and on schedule. Right now, her presence wasn't needed. Vella and Deets had things under control and progress was already being made on her house.

Polly could not leave the boarding house tonight per JD's instructions, so she left a handwritten note for Vella on the dressing table instead.

Vella, sorry to leave on such short notice, but an opportunity to take Martha on a little excursion was made possible tonight.
It will be good for Martha and me to have some light-hearted fun. We will
be staying with a lovely family between Cap Rock and Charles Goodnight's JA spread.
I transferred additional funds to the Texas Bank & Trust from
San Antonio today. You and Deets proceed with the plans. You
always know what to do! If we're gone more than a few days,
I'll send you a telegram. Polly

Polly gave Martha paper and colored pencils before they left. She'd been planning to give them to her and thought the set might give her something to do as JD drove them to the ranch with Newman tied on the back of the buckboard. Low and behold the girl was an artist! She made a shaded drawing of JD, and it was remarkably accurate.

They stopped twice to rest and water the horses. JD fed them handfuls of grain and allowed them chances to graze. One of the stops was close to a bubbly creek providing cold, clear water. They had a picnic there, and Martha waded in the water. Polly had raided the boarding house kitchen and packed an adequate lunch of bread, cheese, hardboiled eggs, and fruit.

When the ranch house finally came into sight, Polly was surprised by its wealth of beauty. It was an oasis in the desert! She'd not been expecting to find anything on such a grand scale as this spacious house and grounds.

It was set in a large yard surrounded by buildings, barns, corrals, paddocks, and beautiful animals. There were even two small cottages neatly kept. This place was its own little community of sorts.

Polly wasn't sure what she expected she'd see at Byrd Ranch, but the impressive ranch house was not it. The wrap around porch scattered with rockers, porch swings, and straight-backed chairs draped with colorful quilts and pillows was a brightly decorated vision to behold.

Ruffled curtains parted in the middle of the large windows. They showed through clear panes of glass. Sunshine was hitting them, and they sparkled like crystals. Window boxes below each were filled with rainbows of wildflowers.

The whining and welcoming of a barking dog announced their arrival. The buff-colored dog ran down the steps wagging his tail. The commotion drew men from inside various buildings. In one of the corrals, three cowboys worked with fine-looking horses. Their heads turned toward the house to see who'd arrived. By all appearances, this was a happy, productive place.

JD called the dog by its name, Gabby. The screen door opened and plopped closing with a pleasant hollow sound. Two attractive women spilled out onto the porch. They stood on the top steps for a moment surveying the company and wiping their hands on the skirts of bibbed aprons. Their smiles welcomed the visitors.

One of the women said, "Grey got the telegram letting us know to expect company today. We have a grand supper planned! It will be like a party." There was laughter in her voice.

"Please, JD, introduce your friends."

He removed his hat and slicked his mop of thick, unruly hair back from his face.

"This is Ms. Melody Potter from San Antonio, and her traveling companion, Martha Wheatley. They need a place to stay for a spell. This is the best place, I figured."

Belle Byrd stepped forward. "JD, I wish you'd brought your family along too. Last time we saw Judy and Hazel, those girls were growing like weeds!

"How's Lilac feeling lately?"

"Tired some, actually a lot tired, and hungry all the time! I may have to take an extra job just to keep food on the table," he joked.

"Melody, what a lovely, musical name, like the patter of a gentle rain! My name's Belle. This is Mary Ann."

Mary Ann stepped down off of the porch and held a friendly hand out to Melody. Then she directed her attention to Martha and spoke warmly to the girl.

"Sari and Maisy, our girls, are going to be so excited to have you visiting, Martha. You look about the same age as them. Do you ride Martha?"

The girl's eyes sparkled. "Yes, Ma'am, I can ride a horse."

"Well, I'm sure the girls can find a horse for you to ride while you're here." Mary Ann spoke encouragingly.

Belle spoke up, "Oh, JD, you'd better be hungry! We're having fried chicken and a chocolate layer cake tonight in your honor!"

JD spoke up, "They're my favorites! By any chance are you making biscuits, peppered gravy, and mashed potatoes?"

Mary Ann smiled, "Well of course! You'd better believe we are!"

Polly saw Martha's reaction to the menu. She was still thin as a rail, but Martha had an appetite. For the first time in her life there was plenty of food available.

Eddie Schmidt, you'll never touch this beautiful creature.

If Polly had to kill the bastard herself, Schmidt would never get a chance to spoil this child's future. She'd not killed a man before the stage was ambushed, but now, she knew she had the courage to pull the trigger on an outlaw.

CHAPTER 19

BACK AGAINST THE WALL

~Eddie Schmidt

Sitting in the Shot 'a Whiskey Saloon nursing a beer, Ed Schmidt burped up a scorching, acidic sourness and belched it out loudly. The miscreant had been suffering with a burning gut for days. The painful malady was a direct result of the ill-fated stage holdup.

He'd always been a bully and a coward. Now, paranoia dogged him day and night. He imagined every person in his hometown of Spur could guess what he'd been up to just by looking at him. Eddie was suspicious of anyone glancing in his direction. Anxiety kept his eyes scanning the smoky room of the saloon for trouble. If anyone even glanced in his direction, his body responded by breaking out in a cold sweat.

Ed hadn't intended to take part in such a recklessly dangerous and public crime. Sure, he fancied himself an outlaw and was proud of it, but he was in over his head.

Robbing a stage full of passengers and loaded with gold coins wasn't anything close to small potatoes. Things had gotten completely out of hand, and people ended up dead. He could almost feel the noose tightening around his neck and choking off his air. He had landed himself in a heck of a mess this time!

Keeping his back pressed against a wall had already become a habit. He couldn't afford to let anyone get the drop by sneaking up on him from behind. His chair was tipped back on two legs solely for the purpose of making him appear relaxed and for the advantage the angle afforded. He scanned his surroundings nervously and watched the front and back doors for comings and goings.

Fear and dread had become Ed's ever-present companions, and he felt as nervous as a one-eyed tomcat. The chance was great he could be connected to any number of crimes, but the Overland Stage heist was by far the biggest.

Ed figured it was best to act normal and be seen hanging around Spur since people were used to him being here. Someone might think it strange if he suddenly disappeared. It seemed like a good place to hide in plain sight.

When Alex started letting him ride beside his men, it stroked Ed's ego. He'd jumped at the chance to work for such a famous desperado. What a mistake! Where had Johns been when all hell broke loose? From the very beginning of the ambush to the end, John's was not there. He was someplace else safe and out of sight.

What a fool he'd been to follow this man, and it was too late to simply walk away from the felon. Ed had seen and done too much already. Alex Johns might have him killed if he tried to leave the gang. The Overland Stage Line heist could put every sheriff in Texas gunning for Ed.

Once the killing started at the stage, he smelled his goose cooking. Murder could get him hung even if he hadn't pulled the trigger. He'd only carried the money back to Alex Johns, but blood was on his hands just by being there. Kriss and Charlie Shotgun were good old boys, and he knew the shit had hit, watching them get shot.

Ed was used to being a pile of unscrupulous scum, but he'd always avoided having the law put paper out on him. There'd be a cash reward on his head for robbing the stagecoach if he was identified, and murder meant every bounty hunter in the west would be hunting for him. It would be hard to find a crevice in Texas to hide.

Before his life had gone to shit things were looking up for him. He'd sent away for a mail order bride. Oh, he didn't intend on marrying her, but he had a plan. Luck had never ridden with Ed Schmidt, and there was still no sign of a change yet.

He hadn't given up on getting his hands on the girl. As soon as she was in his clutches, they'd leave this territory together. What a pleasure he'd have with the bitch first, then he'd sell her services to the highest bidders. He'd live off the revenue she earned on her back.

The flapping, noisy, hinges at the street entrance into the saloon drew his attention. The sunshine's backlighting reduced the person's form to a black silhouette. He could definitely make out the figure of a lady, but it was impossible to see the defining features of the newcomer.

He wasn't the only one staining to see her either. Curious men twisted in their chairs or lifted heads from card games to see what woman would enter this den off the street. A hush spread across the crowd like a blanket as the curvy outline of a woman stepped deeper into the room. It wasn't every day a real lady came into a saloon for a drink filled with bastards.

With her head held high and her back straight as a ramrod, she made deliberate measured tracks to the bar. She stopped in front of Harpy with her back to Ed, and he had no idea who she could be. The woman and Harpy talked with their heads together and bobbing for a few minutes. Then she turned around and nailed her eyes directly on Schmidt, and the shock almost launched him from his seat.

He'd had a nagging hunch the two were discussing him, but now he knew for sure. The rhythm of his heartbeat ratcheted up more than a notch. It was beating as fast as a cornered cottontail's heart. Probably his most defining power came from being mean as a snake, but he was also a lowdown, yellow-bellied, bullying coward with no morals. In a tight spot, he'd do anything to save his hide, anything!

They stared at each other for a long half minute before his nerves gave way, and he involuntarily broke eye contact. He hated his weakness, but he recognized who she was from across the room. He suspected fear registered on his face, and the reflex of disengaging his eyes first was enough to make him look guilty. He was scared to death to the bottom of his worn-out boots.

Quickly, turning back to consult with Harpy, she shoved off and fled the Shot 'a Whiskey through the same creaky batwing doors she'd entered. He waited for as long as he could sit still without exploding before walking up to the bar slowly, trying to act indifferently for the purpose of gleaning information.

"What'll ya have, Eddie?"

"Gimme a beer, say, who was the woman who just left?"

Drawing his beer, Harpy shoved it over to Eddie and collected his dime without ever looking at him. He stayed busy with other customers lined up at the bar. Ed followed him up and down the length of the bar as Harpy kept moving, ignoring Ed as long as possible before answering his question.

Eddie feigned patience while Harpy concentrated on polishing the top of the bar with a rag, drawing beers from the tap for customers, and collecting their coins. Without acknowledging Ed, Harpy gathered emptied glasses and filled nut, cracker, and pickle dishes.

"I asked you who the woman at the bar was?" He repeated the question with an edge to his voice this time.

"Don't know her, Ed, jus' seen her around town."

"Did you get 'er name?

"Nope, didn't ask."

"Well! What did she want?"

Harpy stopped his work and looked directly into the man's face.

"She wanted to know the price of a middle-of-the line bottle of whiskey, said she's gonna have a pardi soon. That's all I know."

With this fictitious answer, Harpy threw the rag into the dry sink. "I gotta go to the backroom 'n' git supplies to restock the bar."

Eddie knew he'd gotten all out of Harpy he was going to get. He downed his beer, wiped his sleeve across his mouth, and quickly took the back way out of the saloon.

What in the hell am I going to do now?

Ed Schmidt hadn't believed one word out of Harpy's mouth. His mind was working with serious and heavy things to ponder. He'd recognized the woman's face from the stage robbery, but he thought she'd been killed. When he rode away, she was lying on the ground, not moving, and her clothes were all bloody.

Today, he knew two things for certain. She was definitely alive, and no woman from the stage robbery was going to walk him to the gallows.

CHAPTER 20

COLD BLOODED KILLER

~ *Ed Schmidt*

The next day, after a sleepless night, Ed Schmidt got wind the marshal rode out of town before daybreak escorting two women. One of them was older and from the description he heard, it was the woman he was trying to locate. He'd decided he would kill her, and the sooner, the better. The description he'd gotten of the blonde girl sounded like the one he'd seen her with at the robbery,

A very jumpy and tormented Ed started asking questions around town and found out the lady he was looking to find was Melody Potter. She was staying at Mable's Boarding House. Inquiring at Mable's place the old lady was tight-lipped as a river clam with details, but he did find out Potter and the girl were sharing a room there.

Eddie came across one of the hired girls hanging out wash behind the boarding house. He mustered what charm he could and struck up a conversation. With a little sweet-talk applied, she was more willing to talk than the old woman. He enticed her to giggle as he playfully doled clothespins out one at a time, teasing the naïve little twit.

He was irked to learn the pretty blonde girl was the one and only Martha Wheatley. She was the skirt he'd sent money to buy a ticket. Ed could have grabbed his mail order bride right off the stage. She was so close he could have reached out and touched her. He owned her!

Damn, double damn! My mail order bride is here! Men will put down their money for an hour with her. I'll be rich! I'll be golly darn rollin' in money!

The wash-girl was more than happy to chatter as long as the clothespins held out. She said Ms. Potter and Martha left early this morning on a trip with the marshal. She didn't know how long they'd be gone or where they'd gone. The hired girl did know they left with three bags.

Eddie had no qualms about killing the woman. It had to be done. He'd hide her body, and at the same time, get his hands on little Miss Martha. It would be like killing two birds with one stone! Ed's intended was way prettier than he'd hoped she'd be. It made him a little regretful he had no intentions of marrying her.

Where could the marshal be taking the two women? Where? I've got to know!

He paid a visit to the aged hostler at the livery, but the old man couldn't recollect many details. The marshal rented a buckboard from him and tied his black to the back of it. The outlaw didn't offer to mention his reason for wanting to know the marshal's business, and the old hostler didn't ask.

He knew nothing about any women, but he'd been assured he'd get his rig back. Marshal didn't say anything else the hostler could recall, but he did say he was on his way out of town. He had no idea which direction the marshal took out of Spur or who went with him.

It was imperative Ed find out exactly where the marshal

went. He was so frustrated he was no closer to getting this particular information. The urgency to find what he needed to know was making him frantic. Time could be running out. Staring down the street an idea suddenly hit him. The telegraph office was off yonder sitting all alone at the very edge of town.

There was a good chance Stearns sent a telegram ahead to let someone know he and the ladies were on the way. If he did, Ed could find out who received the message and what it said from Todd.

Todd was serious as a heart attack about his job, so Ed knew it'd take high-handed tactics to get confidentialities from him. He'd always been a stickler for rules and secrecy even as a kid, but he never liked pain. With the right persuasion Spur's telegraph operator would spill his guts.

He headed his horse to the small, unpainted Western Union telegraph office and opened the door quietly. He reached inside and grabbed the sign off a peg, reading, **Be Back Later**, and switched it with the **Open** sign presently hanging above the front door.

Todd was concentrating on an incoming message. Without even looking up from his work, he proceeded to click off a return answer immediately. He hadn't acknowledged hearing someone come inside. Todd had no idea yet just how bad his day was going to get.

Finally, satisfied his work sent correctly, he turned in his swivel chair, asking, "What can I do for you?" When he realized it was Ed Schmidt, the pleasant welcoming smile dissipated.

"Oh, it's you."

Ed knew stuffy Todd all too well. He was older than Todd, and they'd attended the one room school together as boys. They'd never been friends, actually, more like enemies. They were polar opposites on the chain of human beings.

Todd always came to class clean and shined with his

homework neatly done. He was smart, had an amiable disposition, and all the kids and the teacher loved him. His ma packed his lunch bucket with good food and treats like sugar cookies. Ed would steal from it whenever he had the chance. The only bad thing about Todd's life as a kid was being terrorized and bullied by Eddie Schmidt on a regular basis.

In contrast, everything was wrong with Ed's existence. His clothing was tattered, and he wore no shoes even in the winter. He was dirty and smelled bad. He had sleep in his eyes and wore a frown. The kids were afraid of him. No one wanted to sit by him or play with him, including the teacher. The best thing about Eddie's life as a kid was terrorizing and bullying sissy Todd.

It was a fortunate day if Ed had a piece of bread with bacon grease smeared across it wrapped in old paper to eat at lunchtime on the playground. There was no ma at his home to love him or fill a lunch pail with care. His pa would rather beat him than look at his son.

School was no better for him. He only suffered exclusion and more neglect. Hate boiled inside of the boy for everybody.

"I don't see much of you in here. What do you need? Do you have a message to put on the wire and the money to send it?"

"No, Todd, no message except for you. I need information, and I'm figuring ya have it."

Todd's eyebrows raised in suspicion as Eddie stepped around the counter invading his sacred space.

"This is simple, Todd, so don't make it complicated or you'll be sorry. The marshal rode outta town this mornin'. All you've got to say is where he went, and I'll leave."

"Ed, I wouldn't know."

"Well, I don't think yer tellin' tha truth. I warned ya not to make this hard, just keep it simple. I'm figuring Stearns paid ya to send out a message fer him, and ya know exactly where he is. I'm sure the telegram was to a name and location. Ya know exactly what it said too!"

"Please, Ed, don't ask this of me. Try to understand customers' messages are private, and I'm sworn to secrecy. Besides, I can't remember each message coming in or going out from one day to the next. Yesterday was a very busy day in this office."

The outlaw reached out and twisted Todd's ear as hard as he could and pulled until the skin attaching the meaty part to his head ripped. When the lobe of his ear tore and a line of blood ran down the man's neck, something primal snapped inside Ed Schmidt's mind. He continued pulling until he'd lifted him almost out of the chair.

Ed loved hearing Todd's scream of pain and panic. He'd forgotten how much fun it was to hurt and torment Todd.

"Ow, ow, ow, please, Ed, let go, ok, ok, he, he, I'll tell you, was taking some witnesses to Byrd Ranch!"

"Good boy, Toddy!" Letting go, he praised him, and patted the small man on the head.

"I had a dog obedient like you when I wus a boy. I don't recollect I liked him much either. He was a coward, afraid of his own shadow. I don't admire a show a weakness in man er beast."

Todd's eyes grew as large as saucers when Ed drew his pig stabber out of his belt and flashed it in front of his face. Before the poor man had a chance to cry out, Eddie grabbed him by the hair and neatly slit his throat from ear to ear. Ed laughed out loud to see Todd's mouth open forming a perfect "o" and his eyes staring, wide open, and his neck grinning.

He felt a thrill to see Todd slumped back in his chair, and it gave Ed a hilarious idea. He rotated the seat around until he was facing the wire transmitter. Then he propped his right hand on the keypad, so he appeared to be tapping a message. The slit in his throat had bled out on the front of his shirt. The scene pleased Ed immensely.

He turned to leave but turned back after another idea hit him. Ed grabbed Todd's lunch bucket his loving wife had no doubt packed for him.

"Well, Toddy, looks like lunch is on you one more time!"

He locked the building, with the **BE BACK LATER** sign on the door banging slightly in the wind. It seemed appropriate somehow. What a kick it would be to witness the horrified reaction of the first person to walk in and find Todd.

There was no way of gauging how long it would be before his body was discovered. He might sit in his chair most of the day. Wouldn't it be something if his wife or one of his kids came looking for him! It would be a bonus of sorts.

Ed had no time to waste hanging around here though. He had the information he needed, and some citizen might discover him. A long ride to Byrd Ranch was ahead of him. He had to deal with silencing the woman and grabbing Martha Wheatley as soon as possible.

My very own Martha Wheatly!

CHAPTER 21

POLLY'S DILEMMA

Polly followed Mary Ann into the barn to see Grey and JD embark on a day of scouting. As long as the marshal was out this far, he'd take advantage of the logistics and look for signs of Alec John's gang. He had his map marked with the locations of hits as they were reported, and the number of men visible at each hit. In some cases, witnesses knew which way the thieves rode out, and the directions of exits were marked with an arrow.

If the men found no leads, they'd be back for supper, but if they found something worthy of pursuit, they could be on a trail for however many days it took. The two women feared for the men for different reasons. Mary Ann was concerned for her husband and good friend. Polly was worried about her son possibly facing and killing his own father unknowingly.

Polly was struck with the overwhelming urge to reveal the truth to JD about his parentage before he left. What if Alex shot and killed JD instead? How cruelly ironic it might come down to this after all these years of silence. The paths of father and son quite possibly could be barreling toward intersecting at crossroads.

A showdown between these two men who operated on opposite sides of the law could happen at any time. Why did it have to be now when Polly was gathering the courage to expose her identity and explain all the details to her son?

He'd already mounted Newman. The big black was pawing at the ground ready for the signal to get the show on the road. There wasn't time to relate such a complicated family saga before JD rode away! Polly couldn't possibly talk fast enough to unload the tangled mess and make sense of the multiple tragedies. It was too complex, and she couldn't do such a thing to JD this morning.

Even given the perfect timing, he would have trouble understanding they were both victims, and she hadn't just deserted him. The intricate components of deceit weren't meant to be aired and sorted out in front of strangers if there was a chance her son could forgive her.

She had to talk to her daughter-in-law, Lilac, and bring her up to speed first. The two women were as close to each other as any mother and daughter. Lilac had no idea she wasn't still back in San Antonio. There was also the hitch, she only knew her as Aunt Polly.

She needed Lilac's support before she faced her son. JD's wife, if she was willing, could soften the blow and hopefully influence how he handled the truth. Since Polly was stuck on this ranch, there was no other choice but to put everything on the back burner.

Both horses were stomping their front feet anxiously to get on the road. She'd pray the men responsible for the stage holdup and murders would not be found today. The lawmen had a tip Alex Johns was the gang's ringleader. New Mexico had recently released him from prison, and he'd been sighted heading this way a few weeks ago. They also figured Ed Schmidt was knee deep in this too.

Polly held her head down and was wringing her hands so tightly her knuckles were getting sore. The stress of her thoughts debating back and forth between keeping her mouth shut or stopping the lawmen from going had given her a headache.

"Wait! JD, wait!" she called out to him just as the two men rode away.

He didn't hear her. A cloud of dust had already engulfed them. It rose higher and higher around them as they galloped away. Her futile attempt was reduced to fragmented syllables and lost.

Mary Ann heard her words though and was staring at her. Polly picked up her skirts and ran to the house as fast as her feet could carry her. She didn't want to explain and answer Grey's wife's questions, and she didn't want her to see the tears.

Polly ran up the stairs, falling into her unmade bed. She pulled the covers completely over her head. When Mary Ann checked on her. Polly told her she was suddenly so tired and had a headache. Then she remained on the soft feather bed.

Polly felt wrung out from stress and fatigue, and she hadn't taken time to rest properly. She'd had a string of tiring experiences one after the other since leaving San Antonio,

The early start yesterday on the buck board fleeing to Byrd Ranch, seeing JD ride away this morning, rescuing Martha, and the stagecoach robbery added up to a break down if she was a lesser woman.

As if these were enough, she took this moment to freak out about witnessing innocent people being murdered and the fact she'd gunned down two of the outlaws herself. And, whether she'd admitted it to herself or not, she was continually fretting over Kriss and remembering the two bullets in his chest. She didn't even know if he was still alive.

His daughter and son-in-law came and took him to their homestead several miles away to recuperate and get his strength back. Polly hadn't seen him since the morning after the shooting. The town doctor had taken over his care from there.

When Belle came to check on her, she encouraged Polly to take the whole day to rest in bed. What kind people the Byrds were, all of them! She decided to count her blessings one by one to calm her misery and fears.

At least, Martha was on the road to happiness with the start of rosy cheeks, putting on weight, and laughing like a young girl should. The new clothes and pretties she'd packed into Martha's new tapestry bag were mostly unworn. Martha wanted to dress like her new friends, Maisy and Sari. They had outfitted her with britches, a shirt, a hat, and boots they'd outgrown.

This was the only opportunity she'd ever had to talk and play with girls close to her own age. She'd made two good friends in Maisy and Sari Byrd. They were so sweet to her, and Martha fit right in on the ranch.

Martha knew how to work too, and she gladly fell into helping the girls with their chores. With two extra hands to whip through the tasks faster, they had more time to ride freely off with picnics Belle packed. They'd be scarce around here until suppertime. The adults didn't expect to see hide nor hair of the three until then.

She knew Stone and Clay would meet the girls after their work was finished. The two boys sounded like a couple of wild horses when they burst into the kitchen downstairs. Polly heard them. Belle had told them to grab the grub sack sitting on the kitchen table. She'd already packed it for the boys!

CHAPTER 22

———◆•◦✦◦•◆———

THE BLOODY TELEGRAM

From the barn, Smith noticed a thick, boiling curl of dust headed his way. Very soon, he could make out a horse and rider. The rider came barreling into the yard almost making his horse slide to a stop before dismounting.

Smith recognized the young man who worked at the telegraph office in Cap Rock. Smith was standing in front of the barn between chores and walked forward to offer a friendly greeting.

"I have a telegram from one of the deputies in Spur, came off the wire over an hour ago. It's addressed to the territorial marshal at Byrd Ranch. Where can I find him?"

"JD and my brother rode out together early this morning. Give it to me, and I'll decide if I need to go looking for them."

Smith frowned, shaking his head as he read the telegram through twice.

JD

Todd at telegraph office murdered in chair
Found noon today in dried blood
maybe happened Yesterday
town in uproar please advise   bad one   Deputy Vincent

"Lord, have mercy!"

"JD and Grey have a head start, but I'll get this to them as quick as I can. Give me a minute to write a message to send back on the wire."

Vincent, JD left this morning riding
southwest with Grey.
Will find him.   Smith Byrd

"Here, get this out when you get back to town. It's the best I can do for now, but at least the deputy will know I'm working on it. Put it on the ranch's bill."

The boy readily agreed, "Yes, Sir."

Smith tossed him a coin for his trouble. He handily caught it, nodded, and pocketed the paper and the coin. He watered his horse and headed back to the town of Big Canyon at a much slower pace than he was pushing it before.

Prior to leaving, Smith told the women he had to catchup with JD to give him the telegram. He made sure they understood he was taking Stone and Clay with him. He didn't want them to worry about the boys if they were late getting home.

He knew they'd be with Maisy and Sari making time with the pretty, little, yellow-haired houseguest, Martha.

She had those boys in a spin. Any new girl scrambled their brains. Why, they'd flown through chores this morning faster than a hawk swoops down on a rabbit.

Smith wasn't so old he couldn't remember getting excited about a filly. This girl was sweet, and they were fascinated. Sure enough, the closer he came to Frank's grave on top of the hill, the louder the teasing words and laughter grew. He found himself chuckling at the foolishness of frisky pups.

Smith was every bit as good a tracker as Grey, but he didn't have occasion to use his skills often. The telegram in his saddle bag was something JD needed. He'd want to know about murder committed in Spur, and Smith was willing to track him down.

Stone and Clay were still learning to track animals and people, but the two were good at it already. It was a survival skill for any man in West Texas to master. Grey and his brothers didn't miss an opportunity to teach them or provide more practice in following a cold trail.

A slight disturbance off to his right caused him to pull his horse up short. Standing in the stirrups, he twisted every which way listening and searching for whatever had drawn his attention. Things all around him had gone strangely still, and he had an uneasy feeling something wasn't quite right.

He just couldn't put his finger on whether he'd heard a noise, seen a movement from the corner of his eye, or both. In his gut, he could feel a slight tension rising, but with nothing more to go on, he settled back into the seat of the saddle and engaged his horse into moving forward.

More than likely, the wind rustled foliage, an animal scurried through the undergrowth, or any number of other harmless things could have caught his attention. He dismissed the chance it was anything other than the environment.

When he reached the kids, they quit their foolishness

and jabbering immediately.

"What kind of tall tales are you kids telling each other up here. You can get into trouble for lying, you know."

They all grinned but admitted nothing.

"I want you three girls to hightail it back to the ranch house lickety-split. Coming up the hill just now, I thought I heard a noise or saw something move. I can't explain it, but I'll feel better knowing you three are at home safe and sound. I'm taking the boys with me to run an errand. No one will be here to look after you."

He saw frowns and heard moans and groans galore from Sari and Maisy, but none of their protests touched his heart nor swayed his decision. He seriously wanted them closer to the ranch house. It'd make him feel better knowing they were there and protected. Smith wasn't convinced he had heard something or someone, but neither was he sure he hadn't.

"Now, Ladies!" he hollered. "Mount up and get going."

Maisy and Sari knew better than to argue with their fathers or uncles when their words were spoken assertively. With no further protest, all three collected their things to leave. He knew well enough they weren't pleased, but he didn't care. No one looked at him, talked, or waved a good-bye.

The boys were a different story. Stone and Clay were fine riding with their uncle. Their chests were puffed up like banty roosters. Being singled out to ride with him was an honor. More and more the two young men were more interested in the business of cowboys than playing with the cousins.

Convinced the girls would mind him and be on their way home soon after he left, Smith rode off with his nephews to pick up the trail of the lawmen. He told them about the murder in Spur, and the seriousness of the telegram they had to deliver to JD.

Stone and Clay were soon engrossed in looking for any

signs left by the two horses carrying their pa and the marshal. The tracks weren't hard to pick up or follow considering the riders were not worried about being pursued.

They became engrossed in studying the ground, vegetation, and reading the subtle indications they were on the right track. This was a great jaunt to refresh and practice their skills. Smith had been teaching them to track as soon as the boys had been old enough to ride horses. Stone and Clay had a uncanny aptitude for it.

CHAPTER 23

——◆◈◆——

BAD IDEA

Headstrong as usual, Sari waited until Uncle Smith was out of earshot to speak her mind.

"I'm not one bit ready to cut our day short. It's not fair we should have to go home just because Uncle Smith thinks he heard something but doesn't even know for sure. Seriously, I'm saying I don't think there's any need for us to be in much of a hurry getting back.

"Ma and Aunt Belle don't have any idea, he ordered us home, and Uncle Smith will never know for sure when we left. There's no one at home expecting us right now. Uncle Smith, Stone, and Clay won't get back until suppertime and maybe not even then. We've got time a plenty to burn.

"Let's have fun a while longer. If we keep our mouths shut, we can totally get away with staying. What harm can possibly be in taking our own sweet time?"

"Sari, when you're right, you're right!" Maisy agreed. "I feel like going for a swim. It's hot today and cooling off will feel wonderful! I sure wish the boys hadn't gone off with Uncle Smith."

"Come on Martha, follow us. You can swim, can't you?"

"Yes, but I'm not the best at it. I haven't had many chances to practice."

This decision was reckless and disobedient. Most impulsive actions based on poor judgements often turn out to be big mistakes. Sari and Maisy have been getting too big for their britches lately. Martha probably didn't know any better because she was getting her first tastes of freedom. She'd go along with whatever her new friends wanted. Totally unaware of Ed Schmidt spying on them this whole time, the young girls were confident they were in no danger.

~Eddie

The outlaw watched as the three girls mounted their horses and rode off, and he'd seen Smith Byrd and two others leave in a totally different direction. The girls made no attempt to be quiet, and he could hear every word said. A herd of elephants couldn't have made more noise than they were making.

There was no need for Ed to worry about being spotted because the careless trio commenced to cackling like hens and gave no attention to listening with their ears. It was easy for him to follow and stay undetected. It was extremely simple. They paid no attention to their surroundings. In this rugged, wild country any number of surprisingly bad things could happen to three lone females.

Eddie had his heart and eyes set on his pretty mail order bride, Martha Wheatley. He figured his rights to her were a done deal. Afterall, he'd sent for her and paid the way to get here. Once he got his hands on his mail order bride, he'd start her training and teaching Martha a thing or two about men. She was his property, and he'd use her himself until she got the hang of her new job.

The others were as sweet and ripe as her. Specific ideas about their usefulness kept rolling around in his head and bumping into each other like pool balls. If he took them too, he could open his own brothel.

Aw, what the heck? I'll just take all three.

He decided right then and there on the precipice of the moment to kidnap all of the girls. The other two were Byrds. He should have thought this notion out more carefully, but then Ed wasn't a good thinker and always acted recklessly.

This had all the components of a huge mistake! The men on Byrd Ranch wouldn't hesitate to kill to protect their women. They had a reputation for being tough, persistent, and taking care of their own. Ed should have been afraid, but he never stopped to consider the consequences.

Ed was one greedy son-of-a-gun, and this trait had gotten him into trouble over and over. His minimal thought processes were always compromised further when the chance to make easy money was involved.

At this moment he only figured, if one whore on her back earned him money, then how much more money could three on their backs make him?

Three women together are worth a fortune! I'm gonna be a rich fellow in fancy duds and smokin' big cigars!

All of his life, Eddie had been controlled by impulses without considering the consequences until the damage was incurred. When things went to shit, like they always did, he could never figure out where he'd gone wrong.

This crime spree he'd been on lately had gone sour, but he didn't know how to get off the merry-go-round. Robbing stagecoaches and murdering Todd were enough to get him hung. He might as well forget about killing Melody Potter. Ed Schmidt had to leave this territory now and go someplace he'd never be found. Kidnapping these girls could very well be just the ticket to his future.

The deviant, knuckle head bit his filthy tongue, to keep from shouting out a big hooray when the girls turned their horses to the swimming hole. The little ladies started shucking boots before even dismounting!

What a thrill to watch them stripping off their clothes, letting garments fly to wherever they landed. In the end everything was shed except for thin undergarments. It was disappointing those remained in place, but Eddie still had a view to relish. The show titillated his body through to his dark soul. It'd been a long time since he'd seen the figure of a female up close, He dreamed about naked women often, but this was so much better than a dream.

Racing to be the first one in the water, the noise was gay, silly, and uproarious. He smiled lasciviously as the girls ran screaming and calling to each other. Each girl took a leap off the bank pumping a set of shapely legs. Entry into the water, made a trio of huge splashes raining drops of water falling like diamonds in the bright sunlight.

The underwear must have been made from thin cotton batiste because when it got wet, the little ladies might as well have been naked! The sheer translucent cloth clung to every curve, nook, and cranny of their luscious bodies. It was totally ineffective as a covering, and nothing was left to the imagination.

The hungry outlaw's eyes feasted on tight, pointed nipples and the mounds of young, firm buttocks. Without even thinking about it, he put a hand in his pants and began to stroke. What a show the innocents were putting on for Eddie Schmidt, and damn if he was going to let it go to waste!

They swam and played splashing and dunking each other all in good fun as happy children tend to do. Then they lay stretched out and sunning on the bank to dry. Their talking and laughing was like listening to angels sing.

This was when he made a greedy decision about where he'd take the girls. He'd take them South through

Goodnight's spread. Marshal JD, the Byrds, and Alex Johns wouldn't find them before they reached the cover of the dense Big Bend country. He'd travel day and night. Plenty of good ol' boys hid out there from the law. He'd be safe, and they'd be willing to pay a bounty for a tumble with fresh women like these.

He quietly made his way back to where he'd tethered his horse and retrieved the pliable rope from his saddle bags and rolls of bandages. Ed would tie and gag them. He'd strike now and be miles away from here before dark.

Ed caught the girls by surprise and abruptly interrupted their tomfoolery pointing a pistol in their direction. Maisy, Sari, and Martha stood up immediately, crossing arms over their bodies in an attempt to hide their indecency.

"Ain't that cute! Tryin' to hide somethin' I already seen."

"I can't kill all of you at once, but I can take one of ya down and then another, so don't move less ya want this gun to go off! I think I'll kill the tallest one first."

The girls weren't having fun anymore. They were frozen in place. Not even Sari had smart mouth remarks to make about this situation, but she did call out.

"Do you know who our daddies are? The Byrd brothers won't sleep until they quarter you! Get on your horse and leave us now. We won't tell our folks any of this ever happened."

"Good speech girly, but it won't work. You're already caught."

He pointed at Maisy. "You there, the tallest, step behind this girl." He waved his gun in Sari's direction and nodded his head toward her. Maisy did as she was told. Aiming his gun at Sari's head he threw a piece of rope at Maisy.

"Here, darlin', tie yer friend's hands behind her, good and tight. I'll be watching to see how you do."

"Well, ya done good! Keep followin' orders and we'll get along fine. Here's another piece. Tie her feet together.

"Now, go over to Martha," he said as he knocked Sari to the ground. She crumpled with a cry landing on her knees hard enough to skin them.

"How do you know Martha's name?"

He laughed, bragging, "This here girl's my mail order bride! I own her. Ain't that right, Martha?"

Martha held her head down and cried, because now she knew who he was. Maisy tied her wrists together and then her ankles.

The man shoved her down so hard the girl hit flat on her face. It would leave a big bruise on her cheek, maybe even a black eye.

He stepped behind Maisy, but she started to run. He reached out his boot and tripped her. She landed on a sharp rock tearing the thin cloth. He yanked Maisy's hands behind her back while she was stunned and tied them extra tight and her feet as well.

"Are you just gonna lie down there and wait for me to jerk ya up?" Maisy rose to her knees and with awkward difficulty managed to sit. She was helpless to pull the rent running down the front of her undergarment together.

Eddie started with Maisy. He folded the rolled bandage until it was thick enough to gag her, tying it securely behind her head. From there he moved to Sari and repeated what he'd done to Maisy. Sari wasn't so easy though. She mouthed off and shook her head making it hard for Ed to get the gag in place and tied. He slapped her face as hard as a man for making him work. It would leave a mark.

"My, my, Martha, ain't ya a pretty little thing? I hit the jackpot for only the cost of postage! I'd say I got a bargain."

"Please," she whimpered. "Let the others go. I'm the one you sent traveling money. I'll go with you. Just leave them out of this!"

"I intended to do just as you say, but then I got to thinking how much all three of you are worth together.

Naw, Martha, they're part of the deal. I done decided."

Tied and gagged, he left them to get hold of his horse and bring him close. One-by-one, he threw each girl, stomach first, over the saddles of their horses. He took rope and tied their feet and hands together underneath each horse's belly.

Leading their horses behind, he headed out. For a while, they made all sorts of angry noises even with the gags in their mouths. Ed was glad when they tired of the effort and things became quiet. Except for moans and groans from bouncing painfully on their stomachs, he could almost forget they were there. Understanding their discomfort, brought a smile of pleasure to his face.

Able to get a good distance away from where they'd started, he felt fortunate to find a hiding place just before darkness fell. He needed to rest. It had been a long day. Building a fire was out of the question because the Byrds surely had discovered the girls were missing by now. The men would be coming so it had to be a cold camp.

Ed dumped the girls in a pile. They were so worn down their noises had become no more than whimpers. Tears wet their cheeks and their eyes alternated from darting around to closing them in exhaustion. They couldn't give him any trouble tonight.

He didn't share the grub left in Todd's lunch bucket, or his own stash of jerky and hardtack, or offer to share his bedroll either. Their horses' blankets were damp from the long ride, but he threw them over his shivering prisoners who were still scantily clad. They were barefoot too.

His heart was as cold as the camp, as he selfishly wrapped himself up in the warm bedroll. Closing his eyes, a thought briefly occurred to him. It was probably a bad idea to have left their clothes littered on the ground by the pool. He wished he'd at least thought of bringing their hats along to protect their faces from the sun. He wanted them to be pretty when he hired them out and not all burned to crisp by the sun.

CHAPTER 24

———◆◆◆◆◆———

MURDER IN SPUR

Grey and JD hadn't made much progress today. They'd wasted a few hours following tracks amounting to nothing of consequence. They were considering going back to Byrd Ranch for the night and taking a direct route to Spur in the morning. They also discussed angling toward the wrecked stage and searching in a continuously widening circle from there.

Decision made, they headed in the direction of the ranch but had stopped to rest and water the horses. When Smith's troop found them, Grey was surely proud of Stone and Clay when he heard they'd tracked them easily. Of course, Smith was keeping his eyes peeled, but he claimed later the boys didn't need his help. According to him, they could have accomplished the mission all by themselves.

JD read the troubling telegram and passed it on to Grey.

"Something is sure strange about this," JD said. "Dang, Todd was a friend of mine. He was a good, solid man in the community. Why would anyone want to kill him? It has to be connected with his job in some way. It made him a vulnerable target, and he didn't even carry a gun.

"If my hunch is right, I figure someone was either scouting for information or looking to send it out. Grey, I have a feeling this murder connects in some way to Alex Johns. I just know it."

"You may be right, JD. Where do you want to go from here?"

"I need to get back to Spur. This telegram says the town is in an uproar. If people panic, they might hang an innocent person in a frenzy for justice. I guess it means you and I are heading to Spur."

~*Smith*

Smith, Stone, and Clay headed home. The sun was vanishing by the time they could see the barn, but things didn't look right. Lanterns were lit and shining. Family and hands were churning around outside which was unusual for this time of day.

Cole rode out to meet them.

"The girls never showed up for supper. They're missing. Qynne and I are ready to ride out with some men to find them."

Mary Ann ran and stumbled from the yard with Belle and Polly close behind. They reached out their hands to steady her.

Mary cried, "You have to find them. They've never been late like this before. With darkness falling, they must be frightened! What if they're hurt?"

Smith soothed her, "We'll find them."

Smith called for hands to saddle up a fresh mount for him. Cole had already picked the hands to ride with him.

"Stone, you and Clay stay here." Smith ordered.

Neither boy had ever disobeyed an order on the ranch, but Stone spoke up for both of them.

"No, Uncle Smith, Clay and I will be riding out when you go. Those are our girls and our friend too, Uncle Smith! Something has happened to them, or they'd be home right now getting ready for bed. Martha must be scared half to death since she doesn't know this country. Sari and Maisy are tough, but we need to get to them."

At first, Smith looked at Stone and Clay with furrowed brows and lines creasing his forehead. He looked like he might reject Stone's words, but then his face relaxed, and he shook his head.

"You're right, Stone, I wasn't thinking. You're coming of age. Of course, you want to go find our girls. Go pick out fresh mounts, and let's get going."

There was further tension when Smith said he'd sent the girls home this morning from Frank's Hill. If they never made it back, something was definitely wrong. He promised they'd bring all three girls home.

Polly spoke up then to share Martha's mail order bride story, the threat made against her from Ed Schmidt, and his connection to the stage holdup. She added JD and Grey already knew about the connection.

Smith, Qynne, and Cole took the lead, and the search party rode first to the top of Frank's Hill since it was the last place the three girls had been seen together. All stayed back as the ranch's ramrod and a hand hunted for tracks showing where the girls left the area. It was hard to single them out since so many prints overlapped with Smith's, Stone's, and Clay's horses. They'd all been on the hill this morning too.

The others stood by their horses in one spot with lanterns lit while the two men searched for signs hoping to answer the big question of which way to go next. Finally, the man who helped shoe the ranch's horses recognized a telling flaw belonging to the back left shoe of Maisy's horse. The three horses had ridden together off to the south.

Almost at the same time, one of the men at the bottom

of the hill shouted out they'd found something. Smith went down to inspect the trampled grass and a recently broken branch. This pinpointed where a horse had been tethered. It was easy to see where it had been ridden off southward as well.

The moon was full and bright now. Everyone put out the lanterns tying them to their saddles. They split into two groups with one group starting south from the top of the hill. It was slow going but they didn't even consider giving up and waiting until morning. When in doubt, one of them would dismount and light a lantern to make sure they were still on track.

Cole, Qynne, Stone, and the others started south from where the horse had been tied, and the grass was trampled. The trail was rougher to follow from there because of the thick growth of vegetation. The broken branches and twigs left behind, however, might as well have been a road map. At some point, Cole's group intersected the trail Smith's group was following also.

Later, a collective groan rose from the men's throats once they all reached the swimming hole and saw clothing, hats, and boots were haphazardly abandoned near the water. There were signs the girls had lain in the grass. Their footprints were leading out of the water. There were also traces of them standing and kneeling along with the prints left by a man's boots. No one had any doubts the girls had struggled and had been kidnapped.

The lunch basket Belle had packed sat untouched. Maisy, Sari, and Martha, or their horses were nowhere to be found. The search party grew quiet. Qynne and Cole dismounted and gathered up the clothing and boots. Hopefully, the girls would need them. A raindrop tear rolled down Qynne's face. She was a Pinkerton but hunting for your own made the job harder. Cole squeezed his wife's hand.

Stone and Clay had continued to search around the

perimeters and called out when they discovered the fourth set of tracks headed farther away leading the girls' horses. The lead mount carried the heaviest rider.

The procession following the tracks of the four horses ridden in single file was somber.

Sometime before daybreak, they had Ed Schmidt bleeding, trussed up like a pig, and bound to his saddle after Cole and Smith had worked the sorry man over with their fists. All three girls were stiff, thirsty, hungry, and shivering. They had bruises, skinned places, scratches, and their ankles and wrists had been rubbed raw. Their thin clothing was ripped.

Cole sent two riders ahead to fetch Doc to the ranch. The girls were hysterical, freezing, and hurt. They'd soiled themselves. All three were traumatized and too scared to make sense about what happened to them.

Bedrolls were used as blankets, and Smith, Cole, and the ramrod each cradled a girl in his lap on the way home.

CHAPTER 25

ANOTHER TELEGRAM

JD and Grey rode into Spur before daylight with the giddy up wrung completely out of their backsides! The cowboys took Newman and Spanish Fight to the livery stable for some well-deserved care.

The boy on night duty must have been a light sleeper. He threw back his blanket in an instant and jumped up from the cot where he'd been lying. His hair stuck out in angles as he roughly rubbed the sleep from his eyes with the heels of his hands.

He addressed the two men eagerly, "Hey, Marshal, Ranger! I know what to do with your horses, brush them, tend their feet, and give them fresh hay, oats, and water. Then, I'll put them rest in clean stalls."

"That'd be right fine of you, Jeffry. They've been ridden hard and need it all. We plan on eatin' and gettin' us some much-needed sleep too," JD said.

Grey tossed the boy a coin, and he caught it in the air, grinning.

They sauntered over to the café first with grub in mind. The aromas of coffee, pork frying, and biscuits baking wafted from the door when Grey pulled it open. JD's mouth watered, and his stomach commenced complaining. It was too early for many to be stirring around town yet, and at least for a while, things were quiet.

He planned to check on Lilac and his little girls, Hazel and Judy, right after filling his belly. Then he'd get a few hours of shuteye in his own bed. It was a reasonable plan until word of his arrival spread. Excited people started pouring into the café. Many different heated opinions flew over the marshal's head in chaos about Todd's murder. Demands were made to find the killer. JD tried his best to listen with one ear while chewing the food set before him and Grey at the same time.

People were talking over each other, some louder than others. He was definitely interested in hearing facts, but most of the words were just pure contrived gossip. He'd have to talk to his deputies and look at the inside of the telegraph office before he started putting facts and pieces together.

When the talkers either left or settled at their own tables instead of standing over his meal, the food had a sight more flavor. He focused on thick, amber sorghum syrup dripping from the fluffy golden biscuits. He liked the way the sticky sweetness coated his tongue.

There was just the right amount of heat seasoned into the ham sausage, and six eggs over easy floated in savory pools of peppered grease. He and Grey washed their food down with three mugs of black coffee before pushing their plates back. Once on the street, they parted ways for a few hours. They were walking in their sleep.

Todd's younger brother was filling in for him at the

telegraph office. He was slower at tapping out messages to send and transcribing the incoming clicks, but he'd do until the Western Union Company sent another clerk to run the office.

JD felt sorry for the boy being the only one skilled enough to sit in Todd's chair right after his brother's murder. A deputy had hired a guard to be in the telegraph office with him at all times.

Ed Schmidt was the only local Grey and JD knew who resorted to brandishing a knife when he got angry. This alone was not proof he'd killed Todd though. There was no evident motivation as to why he'd want to murder him. A man being despicable didn't count as proof of wrongdoing. No one came forward claiming to have seen him or anyone else going into the office or coming out on the day of the attack.

Still, suspicion festered in the back of the marshal's mind. He'd need more before he could pin this evil on Ed, but the notion was strong enough to give Grey and JD a place to start. If it turned out to be nothing, they'd look elsewhere.

Todd's brother jumped in the chair when signals of an incoming telegram sounded. On a pad of paper, he recorded the rhythm of the Morse Code in addition to words he recognized spontaneously. He'd have to decipher the full content of the message when it came to a stop.

The telegraph silenced, and he scratched his head while studying the marks, and once the lead pencil slipped from his fingers and rolled onto the floor. He scrambled to retrieve it. With a sigh he started writing the message out on a fresh sheet of the pad. He wouldn't have to send a runner to deliver it.

Immediately he announced, "Marshal JD, this is to you from Cap Rock."

JD

PROBLEM   ED SCHMIDT TOOK
GIRLS
TIED UP AT RANCH NOW
GIRLS SAFE
NEED YOU AND GREY
SMITH

JD read the telegram and handed it to Grey to do the same. They looked at each other but kept silent. JD nodded to his deputy to follow them outside. He handed the paper to the man for him to read it.

"Well, Grey, if we wanted to find something linking Ed to Todd's murder, I'd say this telegram gets us close to it. He knew I was going to your ranch with Polly and Martha. He killed Todd."

"Deputy, keep this under your hat for now. Get word to my wife I'm riding out again. Keep an eye on my family for me like you always do. Get a woman over to sit with Lilac if she needs help. I worry about her being with child and me leaving again."

After picking up food supplies at the general store, for the long trek back, they collected their horses and left for Byrd Ranch.

Once on the trail, Grey said, "Yeah, Ed couldn't have known you took Ms. Potter and Martha to the ranch without forcing Todd to talk about the telegram you sent to Cap Rock. Ed killed him so Todd couldn't tip the deputies off."

"It's the way I figure it, Grey. I need a confession from him though, and I intend to get one."

The ride back to the ranch was tedious since taking this route was getting old. JD and Grey didn't engage in conversation until JD broke the silence between them.

"I'm sorry Maisy and Sari got caught in this along with Martha. Soon, we'll find out the whole story, but I know you'll worry until we can see for sure they're safe and sound.

"I've been thinking a lot about the twins today. They're growing up fast, too fast. To think about your girls being kidnapped and scared by an outlaw makes me worry about how I'm gonna keep my girls safe from trouble. I bring so damn much of it right to my door."

"Well, I didn't keep mine too safe, now, did I, JD? I was off being a ranger instead of protecting my family once again. First it was Beth's murder and losing the three babies before Sari. Then, I was off chasing outlaws when Barton kidnapped Mary Ann. Later, I left Qynne alone to look after the women and children, and she got shot. I should have been there all the time."

"You're being too hard on yourself. Beth had something' to do with taking abuse without telling you. She could have asked for help anytime, and you know it.

"Barton was a rotten bastard. He'd have nabbed Mary out from under your nose, regardless. Don't forget you wouldn't have Stone if things hadn't happened just as they did.

"And as I recall, Grey, you were busy fighting a roaring fire before it could destroy the whole ranch when Wisteria broke into the house on a killing rampage. Cole was the one who made the decision to leave Qynne in charge because she's a Pinkerton agent. It was a reasonable choice he made. Hurt or not, she did end up saving your family, and she recovered.

"As for Eddie, plenty of responsible adults were at the ranch minding the girls. You probably couldn't have done any better if you'd been home.

JD could easily see Cole and Smith had beaten the tar out of Ed the night before, and as a father himself, he didn't have any quarrel with the beating, not one bit. In the scheme of things, Ed had earned a pummeling from Cole for the terror he'd put Maisy, Sari, and Martha through. To JD's thinking, men shouldn't get away with mistreating or violating women without feeling pain themselves.

He didn't enjoy laying his hands on a man to get the truth out of him, but he was willing to resort to it when all else fails. So far, he'd gotten no usable answers from Ed Schmidt concerning Todd's murder or the robbery. He and Grey had been playing good lawman and bad lawman with him. JD was playing the bad lawman. They were getting nowhere with the act. The criminal needed some well-placed hurt put upon him to make him talk about the things he'd done and knew.

The marshal couldn't get Todd's violent death off his mind. Todd, his friend, was smart, kind, and likeable. The whole town loved him, and his family needed him. If JD didn't believe Ed was the one who'd slit his throat and sat him up like a mannequin, he wouldn't consider beating a confession out of him. He couldn't charge him with his death unless the prisoner admitted his involvement. This miserable son-of- a-bitch should dance at the end of a rope, and JD wanted to be there to watch him swing.

There was also the matter of the Overland Stage holdup too. Melody Potter could testify he'd been there, but she couldn't swear a bullet from his gun was responsible for at least one of the killings. It was possible he'd never feel the prickly fibers of a stout rope around his neck for the holdup alone might not be enough for a judge and jury to agree upon the death penalty.

The marshal had to have specific details about the day

the stage was held up to pin murder on him there. He wanted the names of his compadres, especially the identity of the ringleader. JD and Grey both had hunches, it was Alex Johns.

Schmidt was a coward. JD anticipated he could make the scum sing answers like a songbird and quickly with only a few well-placed blows.

Lucky for Eddie, he passed out cold on the barn floor. JD let him lie until he started coming around. Then he pulled him up and shoved him down on a bale of straw and retied his hands behind his back. His head was swaying in a stupor, and he was moaning with a level of consciousness. His eyes were open and disgusting slobber was stringing from his mouth.

"Okay, Ed, do you reckon you've had enough? Cause if I don't get answers real quick, I'll skin your hide off next."

"I'll, uh tell, uh, I took the girls, but one is my wife."

"Shut up! She is not. Tell the truth! I know about you sending for a mail order bride, but you're not married to her. I have talked to Martha and her chaperone.

"What I really want to know is why'd you kill Todd?"

Ed took in a long, labored breath and let it out the same way. JD waited because he could almost see the man's defeat.

"Scared, the woman at saloon saw me, and she knew I's at the stage. Asked around and, you took her outta Spur. I's gonna kill 'er. I went to find if you sent a telegram 'fore you left, sure nuf you did. I found out where you were going.

I kilt Todd, never liked him no how."

JD looked at the few ranch hands standing around in the barn as witnesses.

"Clean him up, feed and water him, and let him sleep.

Grey and I'll take him to Spur in the morning.

CHAPTER 26

POLLY STEARNS

Polly hadn't intended to reveal her identity yet, but too much was happening too fast, and everything added together was snowballing. Her world seemed to be toppling like a line of dominoes! They'd just have to lay where they fell, and she'd try to put them in order again. Polly prayed the elements of her story would be clear enough for her son to accept eventually.

The time to act had come. If she hoped to sway the outcome of the future, words she held in her heart could not be put off any longer. Fearing the fragile thread joining her to JD might be close to breaking forced her to proceed. She had to stop any chance he might unknowingly kill his birth father, the infamous outlaw, Alex Johns.

If she allowed this to happen, the damage between mother and son might be irreparable. One shot to Alex's heart could equal the deathblow to her own heart. At this moment, she sorely wished, more than ever before, eternal damnation on Alex, her early life in New Harmony, Texas, and the hate-filled bitch of a sister-in-law who was surely roasting in hell's fire.

Could she present the maize of events and reasons for deceit logically?

Supper around the big dining room table in the Byrd ranch house was quieter when compared to others Polly had shared with the family. The smaller children had already been fed in the kitchen and put to bed an hour earlier.

Polly was worried about her forthcoming admissions. It pressed heavily on her mind. Also, the bruised and traumatized girls weren't giggling anymore. Stone and Clay were somber. The whole family was quiet.

Polly cut her food and pushed it around her plate giving the appearance she was eating. Her mind was racing with the words she wanted to say to JD. They were practiced words she suddenly couldn't remember, and words filled with panic. It was now or never for her.

No dessert had been prepared for the meal, so biscuits, preserves, and sorghum syrup were set out with fresh butter. The sweet offerings were barely touched. The men rose to leave the table, and so did Polly.

"JD, could we walk outside? I need to talk to you about something of great importance."

"Sure, Ms. Potter," he said agreeably. "Let's go out the front door so I can grab my hat and gun belt on the way."

On reaching the bottom of the porch steps, she turned and looked at him. "My real name, this is one of the things I must tell you. My name is not Melody Potter."

He lost his smile. "Who are you then, if not Melody Potter?"

"My name is Polly Stearns."

Silence overtook their conversation, and the walk halted

momentarily.

"You must be joking," the marshal said. "Do you know my Aunt Polly? Wait, Are you sayin' you're my Aunt Polly? I don't understand."

"Yes and no, I'm James Daniels' sister. I own the East to West Matrimonial Agency in San Antonio. I arranged for you to marry Lilac. It's the match I'm most proud of putting together. I wanted you to have the best wife, and you got her."

"Why would you come to Spur without contacting Lilac? She loves you, Aunt Polly, and I have wanted to meet you for so long. I barely remember seeing a picture of you when I was just a boy. It showed up on the mantel one morning. You looked to be about the age of Sari and Martha, and I'd never seen it before. I asked Ma about the girl in the paper frame.

"Ma became outraged. She said it was an image of Pa's sister. When I started asking questions about why it made her angry, she snatched it out of my hands and threw it in the woodstove. Pa came in to see about the commotion just as the paper was scorching and curling. It burst into flames, turned black, and was gone.

"Then he became angry and said he had every right to have his sister's picture out. They started yelling at each other and spitting spiteful words back and forth. Pa sent me outside, but from under the window, I could still hear the arguing continue. I didn't understand why they were both so furious over a picture.

"The first time I saw you when you were doctoring Kriss, I thought I recognized something familiar in your face. I'd never forgotten the picture, such a sweet, pretty appearance. After the big fight, Pa started taking me with him to the jailhouse every day after unless I was in school. Ma completely ignored me, but then she'd always held a resentment toward me. I never could figure out what I'd done to make her dislike me, her only child.

"When Pa got shot down in the street, it was the saddest day of my life. I did the best I could to help Ma around the place. As usual, she barely spoke to me, but I was used to silence. Then one day, I came home to find my belongings and most of Pa's thrown outside.

"I got the hint and gathered up what I needed, wanted, and could carry with me. Actually, it was a relief to ride away from a home with no joy in it. She was such a bitter, cantankerous woman. It was the excuse I needed to leave her, and I was old enough to make my own way.

"Not too long ago, I got word she'd killed herself, and I didn't even make the effort to go see to her burying. It was welcome news she was finally dead and gone. A man should feel something for his mother, but I didn't."

"I'm so sorry. She wasn't stable. She wasn't your real mother, James Daniel, but I am. You are my child. I've never been married, but I gave birth to you. My brother saved your life when I couldn't. He married someone he didn't love so you could live. You owe your life to your pa! I owe James for your life and mine. He's the hero in this story!"

Polly waited, looking into his eyes, trying to read his feelings, but, of course, reading another person's mind is impossible.

"But how did this happen? I don't understand what you're telling me! Why, after all these years, have you come back? It was the little boy who needed you! I needed you then, not now."

"The day the stage was robbed, I couldn't put my finger on what I thought I saw in you. Why didn't you tell me your real name then, and why didn't Lilac know you were coming to Spur? She loves you. Lilac loves you, and in her condition, she needs her Aunt Polly!

"You're my mother? Keep talking, make me believe it, and explain. Start with why you didn't tell me about your real name until now."

"Let's sit down. This is a long and complicated story. There are other truths you must hear in the whole sorted story before you make up your mind."

The two sat on a log together under a tree until past midnight. JD built a small fire for light and to hold off the chill. Polly told him of her beginnings in the New Harmony settlement with her devoted brother, James Daniel. She described the strict religious rules and lack of tenderness they lived under. She told of the cruelty and harsh punishments meted out if either fell short in the eyes of the religious sect.

She emphasized the strong relationship between her brother and herself. He always protected his little sister as best he could. There was no love under their roof except for the love the two siblings shared. James Daniel was and will always be her hero.

The more difficult words of the saga continued. This was the recount of what took place setting the trajectory of JD's life on the path he's now walking. Polly had dreaded reliving these painful parts for her son.

"One day when I'd just turned fourteen, a handsome, charismatic cowboy showed up in the New Harmony settlement. He was clean, mannerly, willing to work, and quiet. No one suspected he was a gun slinger, or he had ulterior motives, like staying out of sight. He kept his guns and vices hidden. He was accepted to the extent the elders didn't run him off.

"When he started paying attention to me on the sly, I was flattered. It wasn't a worry we were sneaking around, because my brother and I had been sneaking around for years. It was how we survived. The cowboy mesmerized me with his sweet talk. He told me how pretty I was and gave me little gifts.

"He started coaxing me to meet him in the hayloft under the cover darkness. I was so lonely and starved for love, I allowed him to explore my body and do things, because he declared his love for me. I trusted him, and I held back nothing. He promised to take me with him whenever he got ready to leave.

"One day I realized he'd gone without even a good-bye. He just disappeared, and I felt heartbroken. As young as I was, I had no idea he'd planted a seed within me, and a child would grow. I was just a naïve, innocent child myself. I never knew until ma saw the signs.

"My folks and the community shunned me. I was taken before the elders and beaten. It was decided I would wear a label with the word TRASH written on it. I would stay at home out of sight until the baby was born, and then I would be made to leave without anything, not even my baby."

Tears rolled down Polly's cheeks now, and JD shook his head and remained silent. He waited for her to continue.

"It all came to pass as the elders had decreed. I was never allowed to see you, but I did hear your first cry.

James hid and fed me for a couple of days until I could walk. I'd been pulled up directly from the birthing bed and thrown out the door with an old quilt and a loaf of stale bread into the bitter cold of a wet winter.

"He gave me what few coins he had and said he'd decided to marry one of the settlement girls if she'd take my baby along with him. JD, my brother made a great sacrifice for you and me both. Later, when I'd paid my way to San Antonio with the coins he'd given me, I got word to him where I was.

"His wife made me sign legal papers swearing to never try to see or contact you. I read in the newspaper and found out James had been killed, but by the time I sent word, you'd already gone. Not until after I read her small obituary, did I know where to send a letter to you.

"The rest of this story with all of the reasons of why, how, and the what-ifs can wait, but I do have something urgent to tell you.

"I swear I didn't know the cowboy was an outlaw on the

run until several years after you were born. I read about his exploits in a newspaper and have read other accounts since then.

"When I realized you're dogging Alex Johns, it became imperative I do not wait another hour longer to tell you the truth. Please, JD, please, let someone else kill him. You don't need his blood on your hands!

Your real pa is James Daniel Stearns. Your birth father is Alex Johns.

CHAPTER 27

A VOYAGER

~Polly Stearns

Before daybreak, Grey and JD were in the barnyard preparing to take Ed Schmidt back to Spur to stand trial. He was bound and tied to his own horse. His surly, smart-alecky trash talk leaking out of his mouth had earned him a gag.

I'd overheard last night, Schmidt had admitted to running with Alex Johns gang, and he'd also admitted to being a participant in the stage robbery. He was also facing kidnapping charges on account of taking the girls.

I crept to the barn really early this morning in the dark and now stood in the darkest shadows. No one detected my presence, and I was free to listen and watch. My eyes kept darting between JD and Grey. JD's expression was solemn, and he hardly spoke an unnecessary word.

This didn't bode well for our difficult discussion last night. I wasn't surprised, but his silence unnerved me. My own mind was a rolling stew of thoughts about all I'd revealed to my son in such a short time. I'd had twenty-seven years to come to terms with the past. For JD to hear the truth for the very first time was a lot to digest. He'd had nothing to say about my disclosures, so I didn't know where I stood with him. I understood it was too much to dump on someone all at once. Even a strong, tough man like Marshal JD Stearns needed and deserved time to think through my confessions.

What is he feeling?

For myself, the telling turned out not to be a free release. It cost me more than I could have imagined and left me feeling compromised and exposed. My emotions were standing on shaky ground, pummeled, and ragged.

Sharing had opened the door to a closet full of old skeletons I'd long kept locked away. Once turned loose, their rattling bones in my head were making a deafening noise, and I felt unsteady. Crying might offer me a measure of relief, but the well of tears had dried up years ago.

Never having verbally shared my past with another living soul, baring my soul to JD proved almost too painful to bear. The wrongs and injustices had lain buried within my heart for so long, they'd transformed into a festered, hurt-filled knot. I felt the thick-skinned ball of infection when it burst and ran hot the moment, I started speaking the truth.

It was curious when Grey's sons, Stone and Clay, stepped into my line of vision and approached their father with careful steps. My mind snapped to the present. Clay cleared his throat and spoke up like a man for both of them. At almost seventeen, they were closer to manhood than mere youngsters. Until this moment, I hadn't really paid them much mind. I had only considered them to be mere boys. I hadn't shared one word with them,

"Pa, we've come to a decision. We're going with you and the marshal to escort the prisoner to Spur's jail."

His words were spoken loudly and clearly. I'd give him credit for holding his head up and not faltering. He was representing the brothers as a unit with decided determination. This young man, Clay, was declaring their right to be considered old enough and capable enough to ride like men.

They both stood straight and tall under their father's scrutiny, and I wondered how he was going to handle their stepping up. Neither Clay nor Stone broke eye contact with Grey. They were in a stare down for several moments before their pa let out a breath and answered.

"Well, now, Son, I hadn't given any thought to the idea of you two going along with us. I can never be sure how things will go when transporting a dangerous prisoner. I think it'd be better if you stayed behind on the ranch. You may be needed here."

Clay and Stone didn't waffle on their unified stance. Indeed, they admirably held their ground.

"With all due respect for your experience, we don't feel as you do, Sir. Uncle Smith never hesitated to include us when he and the others were ready to ride off to rescue the girls. We mounted up, didn't falter, carried our weight, and never let this family down for a minute. We've earned the right to see this kidnapper and murderer delivered and locked away for what he's done.

"You, Uncle Smith, and Uncle Cole have taught us many things over the years, and we've followed your directions and orders to the letter without hesitation. One of the important things we've learned by example is Byrd men take care of their women to the end. We need to finish the job and see this through to the end also."

"I can see the merit of your reasoning, Clay. Stone, do you have anything to add to what Clay's said? I'm interested to hear words from your own mouth on this matter."

"Yes Sir, I believe Clay's spoken well for the both of us. We're prepared and willing to take on the responsibilities of grown men. There's still business left here on what we started. We're serious about being included in it."

"Are you, now? I can see you two are sincere and have brought up good points." Grey put the palm of his hand on his forehead and rubbed it down his face to cup his chin in thought.

"JD, what do you think about this?"

Without turning around from his horse, JD said slowly, "Boys gotta grow-up to be men sooner or later, I guess. I say to let them go along. We might could use their help."

"Okay, boys, but I'm agreeing only for you to ride along as far as Spur to get this done. Then you'll have to turn around tomorrow and get back to the ranch on your own.

JD and I will be heading out alone from there to track the outlaws who robbed the stagecoach and committed murders. It will be dangerous, and there may be fighting and killing before it's over. I don't want you to go along because it could turn deadly.

"Understand?"

"Yes, Sir!" Both of them readily agreed to their pa's position.

I overheard the exchange between the father and his sons. Ironically, I'd already made up my mind to take the mare I'd been riding on the ranch and follow far enough behind to not be detected. I wondered what the men would say if they knew about this plan of mine. I had no intentions of asking any man's permission, because I had my own score to settle.

Once I make it to Spur, I'll go straight to Vella's apartment and lie low. She'll help me gather the supplies I need to follow Grey and JD from behind when they leave town in pursuit of Alex's gang. They will not suspect I am anywhere around or intending to handle my own agenda.

Leaving to chance my son might be put in the position of having to kill his own father is unacceptable to me. The polecat is the scum of the earth, and I am set on putting him down myself. I deserve the pleasure.

This tangle is all my fault, and I will not leave it to JD to put the rogue down. When the time comes, I'll be there to end Alex Johns life on my terms. I am prepared to fire a bullet into his heart stopping the pumping of blood through his veins once and for all.

Alex Johns, I hope you burn in hell!

Luckily, I know my way around horses and am riding a sweet, gentle mare built for endurance. I called her Filly, and we are already well acquainted. The first leg of my journey is boring but being uneventful can be a good thing. When I reach town, I will ride to the back entrance of the West to East Matrimonial Agency building on Front Street.

My mind set to once again be a voyager.

CHAPTER 28

————◆◆◆◆◆————

A FORTUITOUS PARTNERSHIP

~Polly

As I'd hoped, Vella was home and welcomed me into her upstairs apartment after we bedded Filly down in the small, four-stall shelter with her one mount and Deet's two horses. No one would question an extra horse being there for the night.

If Vella was surprised, I knocked on her door unexpectedly, dressed in men's clothing, she didn't comment. She'd known me too long to be questioning anything I took a notion to do. We were as close as sisters. She knew my past and present, and I knew hers.

I'd borrowed a sidearm, saddlebags, and a bedroll from the ranch's tack room before I left. My pepperbox was tucked into a pants' pocket. Actually, I'd stolen the clothes on my back off of the clothesline behind the bunkhouse.

I planned to replace them with brand new duds when this was over. I wore my own boots, but I also borrowed a battered hat and a heavy denim jacket hanging on the back porch of the ranch house.

It did my heart good to see Vella. As we snacked and drank tea, the two of us sat at the kitchen table catching up and making a list of food stuffs I needed. Assuming I couldn't risk building a fire, canned fruits and tomatoes, jerky, and hardtack would be my trail fare. The opened grain sack in the shed had about the right amount left in it for Filly's needs.

In addition, I needed Vella to purchase ammunition, a spyglass, and three bandanas. I'd bought a new rifle and left it leaning in a corner of Vella's closet just before JD rushed Martha and me out of town. It would go with me.

Vella left straightway to make the purchases before the general store closed for the day. A front window in the apartment afforded a clear view of the livery stable where I knew JD's and Grey's horses were bedded down. Vella and I would cover the window in shifts until the lawmen came to get their horses before daylight. I'd give them a head start and follow at a safe distance just as I'd done today.

Among other details I'd overheard yesterday were the directions to the gang's hideout. Schmidt had divulged them under the threat of more pain. The camp was deep in the Canyons between here and Amarillo. I knew he'd also admitted to murdering the telegraph operator and had no qualms taking the other outlaws down with him. The waste of a man had also admitted luring Martha here to use her body to make money.

I wasn't the least bit deterred by the men leaving town at 4:00 AM. I had a mission to accomplish and was committed to whatever it took to see my job through. I had the rest of my life to rest in luxury drinking mint juleps. Nothing was going to stop me from protecting my son. I left in the direction Grey and JD were traveling. I'd impatiently given them over an hour's head start.

The sun broke above the horizon, and as it rose higher

unveiled the mysterious shadows of darkness mixed with purple and pink hues. As the lighting became brighter, I noticed something curious.

The tracks of not two but four horses seemed to be headed in the same direction I was going. I couldn't claim to be a tracker, but the softened ground from a recent shower made the prints quite pronounced. Whether the horses and riders were traveling together, I could not discern.

I was puzzled about the possible reasons for the extra tracks. I'd assumed JD and Grey were going alone, but now, I wasn't so sure. Four sets of tracks stayed in perfect sync with each other. Two horses in the lead appeared to be followed by two others. My tracks made the fifth set.

It seemed very surprising and curious to me. I dogged them thinking nothing of leaving my own prints behind the others. My tracks made the fifth set.

By mid-afternoon, the tracks led up a rise, and I could hear a running creek on the other side. I heard the water before I caught sight of it. The four riders must have stopped here to freshen their horses.

I looked forward to getting off Filly's back and hobbling her. A break to graze and drink saddle-free would be restful. My backside and muscles were tender. I'd never ridden as much as I had in the last two days. I could only hope my hide would toughen.

I heard something else besides the rippling creek water. There were voices, definitely voices, but not loud enough to distinguish words. Had I caught up to JD and Grey without meaning to do so, or worse, whoever was following them? Either way, letting myself be seen would be problematic.

JD would insist I turn around and go back which I had no intention of doing, but running into strangers could mean danger. I dismounted, tying Filly to a bush, and belly crawled just high enough to peek over the rise above the creek.

To my amazement, I saw Stone and Clay! It didn't take much intelligence to figure out the boys were doing the same thing I was doing, except for a different reason. They were trailing their pa even though he'd specifically told them, in no uncertain terms, to return to Byrd Ranch when they left Spur.

You young buzzards!

When I slid back so I could stand without being seen, I inadvertently dislodged pebbles clattering down to the creek bank. I couldn't help but be impressed at how fast Stone and Clay drew their sidearms, broke away from each other, and rolled to individual cover. This gave them two places to shoot from and better coverage of the area. I had startled them as much or more than their presence had alarmed me.

Not bothering to be quiet any longer, I yelled.

"Hold on, I'm coming down, I'm no threat!"

"Wait, who are you? State your business." Stone called back assertively.

"You know me, Melody Potter."

I could see the Byrd boys exchanging looks, but at least, they didn't refuse me. I untied Filly and rode her down the sloping path for a face-to-face meeting. The boys stared at me the whole way down.

I beat them to the punch with the first question.

"Why are you here? Your pa specifically told you to go back home after you jailed Mr. Schmidt! He won't be pleased to find out you're following him instead!"

"How'd you know what pa said?" challenged Clay. "I don't remember you being there when he told us Spur was as far as we'd go. Did you ask to tag along?"

"Actually, I was there yesterday morning at the barn, you just didn't see me. I was hidden and eavesdropping. I had my own personal reasons for listening, and no I didn't ask permission. I planned to follow Marshal JD and your pa to find the men who robbed the stagecoach. I'm a grown woman, and I can go and do anything I please without asking.

"Again," Polly asked, "why are you here?"

"We owe you no reason, but neither is it exactly a secret. Clay and I intend to back Pa and JD up if they need help. Those two have ridden together a long time, and they like to go into danger alone. We fear one day they may run out of luck. When they find the outlaws, we'll be there too. This time they're not riding solo!"

I shook my head and threw up my hands. "This isn't a game you're playing out here! You boys could get yourselves hurt or even killed."

"We're too old to be called boys," Clay corrected. "Now, you know what we're doing, but what about you, Ma'am? Why are you following JD and Pa?

"I mean no disrespect, but aren't you a little delicate and inexperienced to be out here on your lonesome? It's dangerous for a soft woman like you to be out this far from town. This is not a trip you should be making, Ms. Potter."

"There are many things about me you don't know. Don't go through life judging books by their covers. I'm not near as helpless as either of you paint me to be. The facts are we've found ourselves here together, and, yes, this trip is extremely dangerous for any of us, including JD and Grey.

"Obviously, we have our own, separate reasons for tracking them. I'm not turning back, so don't ask me. Are you two turning back?"

"No," both Stone and Clay answered emphatically.

"I didn't think so, and I won't suggest it again. You're both stubborn, capable young men from what I've seen, and you drew those guns on me like fighters. The only thing to do is forge ahead together. We'll all be safer for the companionship. I promise you I am very prepared to take care of myself."

We agreed to put away our objections for now and

tolerate each other's company. From the creek the men's tracks became harder to follow because of the ground cover. I quickly realized the brothers were schooled trackers. I was impressed and thought myself fortunate to have them. I would have had trouble navigating the trail from here.

"Did you steal the horse from Byrd Ranch?" asked Stone.

"Well, I prefer to think of it as borrowing since Filly is not just some random horse. She was assigned for me to ride while I'm staying on your ranch. Don't worry, she still belongs to your family, and no, I'm not stealing her. I'm thinking of asking Cole if he'll sell her to me."

"Filly?" Clay asked. "You named her?"

"Of course, I'm quite fond of this mare. She deserves to have a name. She's a noble animal. We get along together like friends, and I appreciate her help. She's gentle, sturdy, loyal, and would give her life to save mine. I don't take our partnership lightly."

Stone responded to Polly's answer.

"Most don't understand a horse has a soul. Each deserves to be given a name and treated accordingly. An appreciated horse will work well when treated with gentleness. A mare such as the one you ride is worthy."

"Ms. Potter," Clay confessed, "I'm sorry for not calling you by name earlier. To tell the truth I hadn't really considered you before today. I apologize for implying you stole Filly. I didn't know you and the mare have bonded." After listening to you, I can see you are admirable and deserve my respect.

Clay nodded his agreement with his brother and tipped his hat to her.

Stone admitted, "I'm also guilty of not recognizing your heart, but I can see you clearly now, Ms. Potter. I truly see who you are. Before, I only saw your fancy skirts and manners, all prim and proper, but I now see a glimpse into the hidden side of you. Forgive me.

"Is it true you shot and killed two men who held up the stage?"

"Yes, Stone, and I would have gladly shot them all for what they did."

"There's more to you than shows, Polly Stearns, much more," Clay replied.

For some reason, I had an urge to tell my new traveling companions my real name. I've unwittingly been following them since I left Spur, and apparently, we're going to move out together. Without an explanation, even to myself, I speak.

"My name isn't Melody Potter but Polly Stearns. I'm not willing to tell you any more than this right now. The story is for JD to tell when he's ready, or maybe he never will be."

CHAPTER 29

THE TIME IS NEAR

Stone, Clay, and I talked about a lot of things since meeting together at the creek. They now called me Polly. I enjoyed talking to Stone and Clay over the next couple of days.

I plied them with questions about what it was like to grow up on a big ranch with strong men to follow. Their stories about themselves were entertaining and so well told. Pictures were created in my mind. Among other images, I saw two toddlers riding stick horses as soon as they could walk.

I heard words of pride aimed toward their pa, Grey Byrd, a Texas ranger protecting innocents who can't stand up for themselves. Trying to be more like him over the years, they learned about firearms from books, observations, and questioning any man who'd take the time with two pesky yearlings.

Eventually, they graduated to cleaning weapons and then to practicing using them safely. Clay and Stone evolved into capable marksmen over time. Pa and the Uncles supervised the use of live ammo. Now, as young men, they could shoot from the ground, standing, off of galloping horses, or while running on foot.

~Clay

Clay had a habit of peeling away and scouting ahead. He was the quieter of the two brothers but more restless. Yesterday on one of his jaunts he came upon JD and Grey but was careful not to be seen. Spanish Flight and Newman were hobbled and grazing while they were making camp. It was too early to stop, so Clay surmised the target was close, and they'd be planning their next move.

Quiet and sly like Clay's spirit animal, the wily fox, he skirted a wide swath around Pa and JD. He rode until he came to a network of limestone canyons where the outlaws were probably lying low, waiting for the heat of their crimes to cool. After stealthy reconnaissance work, he got a bird's eye view of exactly where the bastards were hiding. He saw the layout of their camp.

~Polly

I was impatiently waiting for Clay's return. Stone and I tended our horses and made camp because the sunlight would soon slip under the horizon. Clay rode into camp with a smile on his face and jumped off his horse. Grabbing the nearest stick, he squatted to draw a simple map for us in the red, clay-like dirt. The first point marked was where we sat watching.

"We're here," Clay emphasized.

Then he traced the outline of a star, representing Grey and JD, a few inches away and connected our two locations with a line.

"Pa and JD bedded down here early today, so I figured

they had a good reason for stopping and wasting daylight."

Further away, he gouged several jagged trenches representing a network of canyons. A line drawn from one canyon in particular connected all of us to the outlaws' burrow.

Using the stick as a pointer now, he said, "The fugitives are here, sitting just as pretty as you please, growing fat like hens! All of them just right for plucking and frying."

"The distance from where we sit to the lawmen's camp is approximately two miles. Depending on how we navigate it, the distance from their camp to this canyon is another two to three miles, I'm just guessing the distance because I didn't ride to the canyon from their camp but skirted around it. You can bet Pa and JD know exactly which canyon the outlaws are holed up in, so I scouted until I found the place for myself. It wasn't hard to locate it.

"They're definitely not worried anyone's on their tails. I smelled their fires before I laid eyes on them, so the outlaws are resting easy and eating better than us. I'm glad I had your spyglass with me, Ms. Polly. I only counted six hombres and two women, but there may be more men I couldn't see.

"There was one man standing as a lookout off in the distance, so he makes seven. He must have been bored because his head kept nodding like he was dozing. They've all become too confident and careless.

"I high tailed it back here to report. I'm thinking Pa and JD will ride in before daybreak to catch the dirty scoundrels when they're all sleepy and off-guard."

Stone threw in, "We'd better leave earlier than them and find a place to watch the camp from the rim of the canyon or closer.

"Ms. Polly, you're packing weapons. Are you confident you can shoot good enough to hit something from a distance. There'll be trouble soon, and we may need to throw bullets. We can't know if Pa and JD will go down the grade to get closer to the camp or go through a back door. If I know them, I'm expecting it's their plan to go straight in."

"I'm an excellent shot, Stone, with my long-range rifle and equally accomplished with the sidearm. I told you I can carry my own weight, or I wouldn't be here. You needn't worry about me being a weak link."

"Ms. Polly, are you gonna tell us exactly why you are here? I think we have a right to know."

"I'm not sure about your right to know, but I'll tell you I'm here for only one reason. I'm here to kill Alex Johns."

Stone and Clay looked at each other in silence for a long moment.

"Tell me this," said Stone. "Do you know what he looks like? Do you have any idea who you're going up against?"

"Yes, and yes. He looks like the devil. I've had a long time to think about killing this gun slinger. Don't you worry, I'll get it done!"

~Polly

Saying my intent out loud to murder the gang leader made the danger I was facing loom over me. The reality of what I came to do was heavy, but my determination was even more. I had to kill Alex before JD came face to face with him. I wasn't afraid of dying, only of failing. I swore to myself tomorrow would be Alex John's last day on earth.

"I was too anxious to eat but nibbled on beef jerky and hardtack hoping the food would settle my stomach. My nerves were suddenly sparking. Before I crawled into my bedroll, I made an announcement.

"Thank you for allowing me to ride with you, Stone and Clay. You have been most gracious, and I am grateful to you. Once we reach the canyons, we'll be parting ways. You two have your mission, and I have mine. If we don't see each other again, just know I did exactly what I wanted to do."

It was still dark, but the moon was bright enough I could see both young men staring at me with eyes as big as pool balls. Neither one said anything, which was no surprise.

This was my journey, and I couldn't be swayed from the path I'd chosen.

We broke camp early, talking little. Clay knew the way we should go to avoid JD and Grey. We followed him toward the canyons. We rode hard and stayed in the saddles without breaking.

Keeping out-of-sight and riding in the dark were entirely two different skill sets. Traveling in the day was much easier. It was imperative to pass through the distance unseen, and I soon felt the tension of towing such a fine line between the two was nettling my nerves and making my skin moist. I could feel the breeze causing my dampened skin to become clammy. Apprehension was making my neck ache all the way down between my shoulder blades.

My companions and I dared not speak in conversation, and we moved down wind to avoid JD's and Grey's mounts from being alerted to the scents of our horses. The few miles we traveled now were tediously slow. The sun was just beginning to show its beautiful signs of waking up.

The quiet ride gave me a lot of time to mull over all the information Stone and Clay had shared about themselves and their heritage. No wonder, they had the wisdom of the ages and intuitive abilities. They were part Comanche and part Irish.

Clay had less of the Comanche bloodline and more of the Irish lineage, but he had more native American characteristics than his brother. Stone had more of the Comanche bloodline than the Irish lineage, but he had more Irish resemblances.

Both of their birth fathers had been Frank McGill, a

Comanche breed, but they were adopted and raised by Grey and Mary Byrd as their own children. They were Byrds of the Byrd Ranch Legacy. Mary Ann was Clay's actual birth mother. Stone's birth mother was a Comanche warrior named Aoife.

They'd shared enough of their backgrounds with me to form a panoramic view of their patchwork quilt inheritances. Curiously, I could see traces and glimpses of all three humanities in each of their natures. They were uniquely different, but both smart, clever, and talented. The power and love of the Byrd brand had protected them from prejudice.

The ride was over, but this was just the start of what was to come. From the incline of a rise and the tall grass, we lay hidden on our bellies and spied on the camp. Hardly anyone was moving around down below except for two women just starting to cook. Clay was right when he'd said the men were eating better than us.

Across the canyon we spotted our two cowboys. One rode the black, and the other rode the appaloosa. We'd seen enough and rose from the ground. Together, we made our way back to the horses. By Filly's left side lay a long eagle's feather on the ground directly under my stirrup.

Stone said, "Look Clay, Frank has been here. He left a gift for Polly."

"Who?" I asked, as I was looking around me thinking I might see someone.

"Frank McGill is our Comanche father. He gives us gifts when he wants to get our attention or to tell us something. He has left you an eagle feather, Polly. He is declaring you are a warrior woman like Stone's Comanche mother, Aoife. He is also acknowledging you as a true friend we can trust.

"He says today, you will soar like an eagle."

Clay walked over to Filly and tied the feather to her bridle. It bobbed around in the light wind. He said, "We have never spoken of this connection we have with Frank to anyone. It is between us and our Comanche Father, but because we ride with you as true friends, he has given you a sign.

"Frank will ride with you today, Polly Stearns, and keep you safe. He sees you are a warrior woman riding fearlessly into battle against an enemy," said Stone.

I didn't know what to say, but I believed them both. They spoke with total conviction about the symbolism of this feather. Before they rode away, each lifted his right palm my way without smiling or speaking. For some reason, I solemnly lifted my palm to the brothers in answer.

Then, they rode away without looking back. I felt a complete warmth come over me and was free of all fear. The boys I'd grown to admire left me and rode one way around the canyon wall. I rode the other.

I prayed for them, for their pa and my son, and for the chance to do what I'd come to do. I couldn't right any wrongs, but I could lay one to rest. Somehow, I didn't feel alone.

CHAPTER 30

A GOOD DAY TO DIE

~Polly

All thoughts not having to do with hunting Alex Johns and putting him down evaporated. I was going into this with tunnel vision to reach one goal, murder. Staying out of sight, I rode Filly around the edge of the canyon. Using the spyglass, I could keep track of where the boys were in relationship to the lawmen.

I made it to the side of the gulch until I could see right into the camp. JD and Grey had taken positions far apart to cover the way in and out of the camp. They had no idea they wouldn't be fighting this battle alone. I could see Stone and Clay had also split up strategically.

Some of the Johns Gang would be in eternity before noon, maybe all of them. It was doubtful any outlaws living through this morning wouldn't be captured and taken back to face justice. It would be better for them to die right here on the valley's floor.

With the glass, I looked for someone who might be Alex Johns. I had a child's image of him, from long ago, seared in my brain. A few years ago, I'd cut out a grainy picture of him from a newspaper. I thought I'd recognize him when I had the chance, but I hadn't spotted him yet.

Only a couple of the slimy worms had crawled out of the low tents and crude shelters. One of the men slapped a cooking girl hard on the ass as he walked by to take a leak on the edge in some scrubs. I heard the slap from where I was, so it had to have stung.

The first shot cracked the calm just before dawn. It came from JD's direction. It drew the attention of the outlaws, and men started scooting out of tents and scurrying about like ants. They were all out now to take cover and defend themselves. Guns started blazing in disordered confusion, and the thieves were shooting blindly, wasting their bullets.

At first Stone and Clay just watched. Then they zeroed in and picked off two men from their vantage points. At last, I saw a man slip from under the backside of a tent and make a run for the horse closest to him. There was no doubt in my mind who the rat bastard was! He had no intention of going down with the ship like a good captain. Alex John's was abandoning his men to save his own skin!

This couldn't have worked out more perfectly for me. I'd hoped to get the chance to confront him alone. Filly and I flew in pursuit as he made his get-a-way. No one, except Clay and Stone had any idea I was here today.

I had never ridden a horse so fast. Filly and I flew like an eagle. From a dead run I shot my handgun and hit him in the back of his shoulder. I wanted him looking at me when I killed him. The force of the bullet knocked him off the back of the horse and his gun flew to the side somewhere out of his reach. The freed horse set sail for Kansas!

I praised Filly for her service and patted her neck before I dismounted. By this time, Alex had managed to turnover, but he was hurting and disarmed. He had drawn his knife, but I easily kicked it out of his hand. I stood over him looking down and pointed my gun at his blackened heart.

I could see the sight of a woman surprised him. I laughed loudly. He was older, of course, with a scar on his cheek, but I recognized him, alright.

"Who are you?" he sputtered."

"You don't remember me, do you? I've been wanting to kill you for twenty-seven years. You used me and left me in a bad way. You and I have a son. In fact, he's the one who led the ambush today. He's a territorial marshal.

"I'm Polly Stearns, and I'm the last thing you're going to remember!"

Then I pulled the trigger. He took his last sorry breath on this earth with blood dribbling out of his mouth, and I was glad! It was a good day for Alex Johns to die.

I made a decision right then to leave and not stop until I made it back to Byrd Ranch. The boys might or might not keep my secret. It didn't really matter, but it would go easier on me if they did. I would have enjoyed seeing their faces today when they found Alex Johns with a bullet in his heart.

I only regretted one thing. JD would have to bury him, but at least, he didn't have to plant the bullet that killed his own father.

It wasn't until miles later, to my disappointment, I noticed the feather was gone.

Loudly I said, "Frank McGill, I sure hope you can hear me. Thank you for the feather of encouragement. You have two mighty fine young men."

CHAPTER 31

―――◆―◈✦◈―◆――

RATTLESNAKE MASTER

~JD

Once the clash was over, and all was silent, I began to take inventory of those who survived and those who died or were in the process. Grey and I were still standing, and the nameless men behind the rifles on the ridge had kept returning fire until the very end. In fact, the last shot fired had come from one of them.

As I surveyed the camp from the ground, I had to admit the spit it took for these 'ole cowboy outlaws to fight as hard as they did. They were caught off guard and pinned down, and it would have been easier to throw down arms and surrender. These lawless men didn't have a chance from the get-go with four rifles relentlessly taking apart their warren where they'd felt safe.

I had taken a hit in the flesh of my upper arm and considered myself very lucky the bullet had passed straight through the fleshy part. It never slowed down my effectiveness during the turmoil and was just now stinging. Grey would have to clean and bandage it later.

It was unexpected when shooters in a different location on the rim joined in to help us out of nowhere. I was too busy reloading to ponder the mystery further in the frenzy of crossfire. At this point, I appreciated any port in the storm as long as the newcomers weren't shooting at us.

I identified two weapons in play and followed the trajectory of the shots. They were keeping the outlaws busy, and some of their bullets hit specific targets.

The noise of active fire stopped, and I saw the last two bandits below with guns thrown down and hands up sitting in what was left of the camp shot apart around them. Grey and I waited, looking for any movement. We had to be sure any threat of confrontation was over.

The two Mexican girls who'd been cooking had run frantically into the brush as soon as the commotion started. Maybe they took off and were long gone, but I'd wager on them crawling out from hiding soon. Most likely they weren't part of the gang but only being held to feed and service the outlaws' basic urges. Liberation had to be a welcome relief for these girls.

The instant Stone and Clay made their appearances, I knew who'd been backing us up. I heard Grey curse, but I knew his sons had done him proud today. When boys grow into men, the transition can come on awful quick sometimes. No father can ask for more than to have raised capable sons on the right side of the law.

I touched the brim of my hat and nodded a thank you to them. Then, I turned my back on Grey, Stone, and Clay. I had no intention of meddling in a family matter between my friend and his children.

Then Grey started talking, and I acted like I heard nothing.

"Boys, you could have been killed today!"

Clay answered calmly and logically, "Pa, I know what

you're going to say, but you taught us how to handle ourselves. We weren't killed or even hurt, but JD took a hit. Sir, you, or JD could have been in trouble."

"Well, Clay, you have no idea of knowing what I was going to say.

"I thank you for being here to cover us, especially since everything turned out alright. You both did right good, you did well, but next time tell me when you aren't gonna do what yer told."

"Okay Sir, you've got a deal, thank you, Sir."

"Take orders from JD now and help in any way you can with his investigation. We're not finished here yet. There's still a lot to be done. The stolen money may be around here so be on the lookout for it. There's buryin' to be done too."

Securing the area started with Grey and me tying up the two survivors as soon as we got to the camp. We'd hogtied, gagged, and blindfolded them immediately. I wanted them disoriented when I interrogated the two.

Now, Stone and Clay were rounding up the bandits' horses and organizing any tack they could find. Grey and I were still going through pockets, picking up guns, and unloading them. We scoured shelters for belongings and things of value or interest. So far, the loot hadn't surfaced.

Before the first shot was fired, Grey and I counted eight men, plus, two raggedy-looking young girls who'd run away as soon as the shooting started. There were two of the fugitives alive but injured. We were letting them mellow before interrogating them.

Six were dead or as good as, but Alex Johns was not among them. He must have slipped away during the scrimmage without us knowing. He'd make nine. By the time we can cut loose from this site, he'll be out of Texas!

I'd have to send a telegram to Austin putting the word out Alex Johns, murderer, and thief was on the run, armed and dangerous. Lawmen and citizens in Texas, New Mexico, Oklahoma, and Colorado needed to be on alert.

They needed to know the money from the Overland Stage and Abilene bank hadn't been recovered yet.

Stone and Clay were carrying the bodies to the edge of the camp and laying them out in a row. Grey had ungagged the mouths of the two captured men. He enticed them to cooperate by offering medical care in exchange for information and identifying themselves and the dead.

We separated the two hurting men to question them. Each of us took one, and we traded later drilling them again. We wanted to know lots of things but especially about Johns, the hold-up murders, and the money robbed from the stage. They admitted Johns was in camp this morning when the shooting started but both claimed to have no idea when he got away or where he might be headed.

Afterwards, Grey cleaned and bandaged their wounds for the information and gave them a little laudanum for the pain. They were passed out.

Just as I figured, Las chicas had come back and started cooking. The aroma of beef stew and fresh tortillas made my stomach growl. None of us but the prisoners had enjoyed a hot meal in days. Grey and I spoke broken Spanish, enough to get by. Clay, however, spoke it fluently, so I assigned him to find out what he could.

They were anxious to tell their story and cried.

"Lo harían estado trabajando en campo de maíz cuando los hombres vino y tomó nosotros de padre's granja. Los hombres las golpeaban y las violaban para muchos días. Estaban heridos y asustados y quería madre y abuela. Ellos quería ir a casa a ver a sus hermanos y hermanas. La casa era de varios kilómetros lejos, y Si lo hubieran hecho uno caballo, podrían cabalga desde aquí."

Clay translated what they told him to JD.

"They had been working in the cornfield when the men came and took them from their father's farm. They are hurt. The men beat and raped them for many days. They were scared.

"They want to go to their mother and grandmother. They want to go home and see their brothers and sisters. The house is many miles away. If they had one horse, they could leave here."

JD said, "No surprises there, huh, Clay"

"No Sir, it's very sad."

After eating their fill of the flavorful stew and bread, JD gave the girls four of the outlaws' horses with their tack and several dollars from the pockets of the dead.

JD had Clay tell them to take any food they wanted from what's left and load it on the two spare horses. He sent them on their way with written proof he'd given them the horses and guns. It was hard to fathom what they'd been through at the hands of the criminals, but maybe, in time, JD hoped, they'd be able to heal at home.

Stone and Clay started the chore of digging a mass grave, while the other two started going through all the saddle bags. There were two extra horses to carry whatever they wanted to salvage. JD and Grey sorted things into two piles. Then they helped with the digging and scraping the shallow pit until it was finished. They laid three men across the width with two more on top and covered them up with the dirt and a few rocks.

This was the high price these thugs paid for pillaging the innocent, a stagecoach robbery, and cold-blooded murder. The gold and cash were not found, so it must be lying in a cache where they'd stashed it before coming here to lay low. JD would press the two men and Ed for more when he got back to Spur.

There was still a couple of hours left of daylight when they pulled out with the two prisoners and the two extra horses in tow. They were exhausted and dirty, but the last thing anyone wanted to do was stay another minute in this valley of the dead.

They found a faint trail of bruised grass where two

horses galloped through recently. After less than a half hour, they spotted a man lying on his back in the grass. JD had never expected to find Alex Johns dead, cold, and stiffened in a stage of rigor-mortis. His eyes were wide open, dry, and fixed, staring into the bright, cloudless sky.

Alex's slightly open mouth made him seem surprised to have ended up here. The relentless prairie wind was gusting enough to lift his hair, allowing it to fall back into place to be lifted again back and forth. The constricting of the muscles causing the body to stiffen in contrast to the wind blowing his hair was surreal.

On inspection, a bullet had entered the back of his shoulder and traveled all the way through and out the front. Whoever shot him in the back hadn't intended to kill him. The bullet which killed him had been neatly placed in his chest from the front to enter his heart. It looked like this wound had been fired at close range.

He'd died instantly with the shooter possibly looking directly into his face. Just guessing, JD wondered if it was a killing of revenge. Examining the tracks, the killer had left here at a gallop in a hurry to get away.

Alex Johns' horse was nowhere to be found but his gun was to his right, out of his reach, and his knife was a further piece away beyond his head. It could have been kicked out of his hand and landed in this position. Studying the marks on his right hand, made this a plausible assumption.

Stone and Clay exchanged solemn glances as Clay picked up the eagle feather caught up in blades of tall grass. He tucked it into his saddle bag.

They knew where it came from and would not falter in keeping Polly's secret. They never would talk specifically about her feather, even to each, other until years later. It was enough to know about this warrior woman, gentle yet with brave determination few men possessed.

The prisoners verified this was indeed their ringleader. There was no doubt to the lawmen this was Alex Johns because he had a facial scar matching the one on his wanted poster.

"With all four of us digging and scraping, we'll have him buried in no time and be on our way," Grey said. "We're not bunking down near this man's grave. Too many ghosts are liable to be after him."

Rattlesnake Master was a weed loaded with prickly bulbs similar to the rattles on the end of its namesake's tail. It grew in bunches at the location of Alex John's death and his hasty internment on the prairie.

JD felt these plants made a fitting memorial for the unmarked grave of a bad man. Sweet wildflower blooms most likely couldn't grow in the same soil as a man gone so sour as Alex Johns. This had to be poetic justice.

Looking down at the fallen man, JD felt nothing. He certainly wasn't his father, and he had dishonored his mother in the most unforgivable way. It was impossible to pardon him, so for now he'd have to settle for forgetting him. Remembering the wonderful father he had in James Daniel made it easier.

Even so, growing up JD had always sensed a piece was missing from his life. Pa took care of him while a hateful ma did nothing but feed him. Pa, however, loved him unconditionally and provided him with all a boy ever needed. JD never felt much sting from the woman's neglect. His father taught him to stand up for decency and be a man of honor and vision.

As the men mounted and rode away, JD spit upon the freshly turned mound of sod. Then he mounted Newman and never once looked back. It was finished.

My pa's name is James Daniel Stearns. He raised me, his sister's boy, as his own. Her name is Polly Stearns. I'm glad to know her and the rest of my story.

Stone and Clay hung back, and when JD was out of sight, Clay took the eagle feather from his saddle bag. They stood at the head of the turned dirt marking the grave. Clay bent over and stuck the feather into the burial place of Alex Johns.

"Thank you, Frank McGill," both young men said in unison. Then they mounted and rode away to catch up with the others. Clay and Stone never once looked back.

CHAPTER 32

———◆·❖·◆———

THE HIDDEN TRUTHS

~Polly

olly was fascinated with Stone and Clay. The thoughts they'd shared with her about things were deep. From the time they'd spent on the trail together, she recognized them as knowledgeable beyond their years. Neither had lived long enough upon the earth to be so in tune with man, nature, and spiritual insights. It was like they had been born old.

A high level of integrity lay rooted in their inner compasses for distinguishing among right, wrong, and justice. They worked as a unit with bravery and shared a code of honor. She had bonded to them somehow. Polly felt connected to Stone and Clay.

Polly felt her dark secret was safe with them without even asking it they'd keep it among the three of them. She would never have asked Stone and Clay to overlook her actions or beg them to remain silent.

In the eyes of the law, she was a murderess who'd

planned the killing of another human being. Polly understood full-well the brevity of what she'd done and had braced herself to face the consequences. Polly accepted she could have dues to pay.

The fact Alex John's was a cold-blooded killer did not negate the fact she'd committed premeditated murder outside of the law. She had killed Alex Johns in the same manner as he had lived. It made her no different than the outlaw. Polly knew she might be hanged by the neck until dead if her actions came to light.

Back at Byrd Ranch, Grey hadn't given her any reason to think he knew she'd been anywhere around on the day Alex Johns had met his Waterloo. She was confident the boys had never told of their travels together or what she'd done. Polly felt safe.

JD had not returned to the ranch with Grey, and Polly yearned to go to Spur as soon as possible. She wanted to ride away from the tension and put distance between herself and Byrd Ranch, but her departure was delayed.

A pressing matter concerning Martha's future had presented itself. The Byrds had decided to send Maisy and Sari to a boarding school in light of the kidnapping, and they offered the same opportunity to Martha.

Polly wasn't ready to give the girl up, but she knew it wasn't fair to hold her back either. Martha could learn about the world beyond. Reading, writing, mathematics, geography, Latin, music, art, dancing, and etiquette would open endless possibilities. Polly could well afford the expenses involved, so it was settled.

Plans were finalized, and the girls were enrolled to attend when the new semester started after Christmas. Qynne would see them to the school since she'd been exposed to travel and Mary Ann and Belle had not. Polly could've gone, but she chose not to offer. She was determined to return to Spur. JD and his family were there, and she had been neglecting her mail order bride agency.

A ranch hand drove Polly back to Spur with her horse, Filly, tied to the back of the buckboard. She proudly held the bill of sale in her reticule signed by Cole making the precious mare legally hers to keep.

She hadn't seen or heard from JD since she'd emptied her heart out to him the night before he left to take Schmidt to jail. He'd had time to think about the story, but she had no idea what his feelings were toward her now. At least, he knew what she did, and it was only right. A great weight had been lifted off of her.

Alex Johns and his gang were no more, and the three, left alive, including Ed Schmidt had been escorted by a deputy to Fort Worth and were left there awaiting trial. It was still unclear who'd killed Alex Johns. The general consensus was it had been a bandit with a grudge who'd killed him and gotten away with the money. It was a plausible explanation.

Polly's two mail order bride agencies, both near and far, demanded her immediate attention and kept her too busy to think of much else. The services she provided helped so many lonely women and men connect.

Couples married and ladies moved on to start families in the love and security of forever homes with men to care for them. Polly was very proud of the work of her loyal staff like Vella, Deets, and the other employees managing the San Antonio branch.

By the standards of the day, Polly was more than successful and financially independent. She couldn't stop wondering though what the future held for her.

Where does my life go from here?

Polly had gone to see Lilac. She hadn't known what her reception would be, but she couldn't stay away any longer. By now, Lilac would have heard the whole story from JD, and she would have had time to sort the information out.

She didn't want to blindside Lilac, so Polly sent a note the day before the visit. When she rode Filly into the yard, she was pleased to see how tidy the place looked on the outside. She knocked and didn't have to wait long before little tapping steps were scurrying to the door. The knob turned, and Lilac, with water pooling around her eyes, embraced Polly in a hug.

Lilac whispered into her ear.

"I'm so mad at you! Why didn't you trust me enough to be honest? I would have listened. I love you so much, Polly. Love covers all."

Polly was reassured by Lilac's sentiments, but she didn't have time to respond because Judy and Hazel were bouncing up and down at their mother's feet vying for attention. Their exuberance took precedence over Lilac's words. They squealed in childish impatience, "Aunt Polly, Aunt Polly!"

This made Polly's eyes water as she laughed at the sight of her grandchildren. She kneeled and held the twins closely to her at the same time. She handed each little darling a brightly dressed ragdoll with brown yarn hair braided and tied in ribbons. They had shiny, black button eyes sparkling in the light.

One doll was dressed in pink gingham, and the other in yellow gingham. The gifts made them giggle. As soon as the dolls were in their hands, the twins hollered a thank you as they ran off to play.

Lilac served tea and cookies at the table. She left with a refreshment tray to take to her girls. When she came back and sat at the table an awkward minute passed before she started to talk.

"I've missed you so much Polly, you have no idea how much. I can't believe you're going to live here in Spur. You're as dear to me as any mother could be, and you are my husband's mother, and the grandmother to my children.

"I know JD hasn't made an effort to see you yet, but he will, I promise. He's not angry, it's just been a lot of information to digest, and he wants you to get settled first.

"JD told me everything. I can tell he's mulling over your story along with things he remembers from his childhood. Your brother, James Daniel, was a devoted father, and JD has only good recollections of him. I can also tell you he's glad Alex Johns is done and forgotten.

"It saddens him to think how badly you were treated and how you must have felt abandoned and alone. I can't tell you exactly what he's thinking, but I can only tell you, JD wants a family relationship with you. Polly, you are his only mother.

"Lately, JD stands and looks silently out the window for minutes at a time, and he works outdoors more. In his own way, he'll come to you. Be patient and wait. In the meantime, he has no intention of keeping me and our children away from you.

"As far as my feelings, nothing has changed. You are my mother-in-law. Be clear, in light of all I've said, you know my first allegiance is to my husband. You taught me to respect the natural order of things in a good marriage.

"JD's a good husband and father, and I love him so much. Don't you worry, he'll be the best son! This will turn out well between you and him."

By the time Lilac was finished saying what was on her heart, the women were both crying. JD wasn't angry. What a huge blessing! She'd bide her time and give him space. She'd grieved over what happened for forty-two years, but JD had just found out. He had the facts to work through.

When the dust settles from this chapter of her life, Polly thought about taking her own professional advice. She might put a line out and test the water for herself. Maybe she could reel in a suitable man!

Just the ludicrous thought made her laugh out loud. It was totally and utterly ridiculous! She'd only met one man she'd even consider since coming here to West Texas. She didn't even know where he was, and she was afraid he might already be dead.

CHAPTER 33

CUTTING THE RIBBON

Deets and his crew were making steady progress on Polly's new Victorian style house. Soon the downstairs would be ready for Polly, the cook, and his wife to move into their downstairs quarters while construction on the upper bedrooms for boarders would continue.

A virtual beehive of activity swarmed the land Mary Ann Barton used to own. It was ironic Vella bought the land from her before Polly and the woman happened to meet later.

Construction on both the outside and inside was continuous and often noisy. A few workers were hired just for landscaping, fence building, porch building, and gardening. Deets had been respectfully planning around the grave and memorial of Mary Ann's mother. It made Polly feel more a part of the Byrd family.

A temporary outdoor tent kitchen was operational for now, and the cook and his wife had been hired to feed all the workers breakfast and a noonday meal. Later the cook would move into the big house with his wife. She'd be the housekeeper. Along with salaries, a small apartment would be included.

Delivery wagons were in and out with supplies. They were unloaded and put in the areas needed or stored out of the weather for later use.

A barn with an attached stable as well as Deets' cottage, where he now lived, were already finished. Deets had found he loved this part of Texas and would be staying in Polly's employ here. He was already corresponding with some of the agency's mail order brides. Polly was delighted he was staying.

Polly still lived quite comfortably at Mabel's Boarding House. She was no longer keeping such a low profile in Spur. She was free to use her real name. In most ways she could be herself, except no one but Lilac and JD knew she was more than his aunt.

Polly took her meals with the rest of the boarders. She'd made the acquaintance of a man staying there also. He wasn't the kind of man she admired, but occasional conversation with Ted Rhymes made a tiny dent in her loneliness. She was careful not to lead him to expect more.

They'd taken an after-supper walk together once, enjoyed chatting before meals, and one Sunday morning they attended church together. He was a self-centered man who talked about himself mostly. He professed to be in business, but for the life of her she couldn't nail down what kind of business.

Mr. Rhymes asked too many questions about Polly's business enterprises. Though he was persistent in asking, she was too smart to talk about her assets with strangers, especially men. She was tight-lipped with Ted, and he was beginning to pressure her and make a nuisance of himself.

The West to East Matrimonial Agency was finally open for business. The eye-catching storefront sign was hung and creating quite a buzz in town. The big grand opening was only one week away, and it would be similar to a street fair ending with a community dance. Nothing drew a crowd like a chance to have fun and take a break from the drudgery of everyday life on the prairie.

Vella was the chairman of planning and coordinating the festivities. She involved as many townspeople and others in the outlying areas as possible in the big ribbon cutting event. It was good politics. Deets used carpenters from the house site to put up a simple speakers' platform in front of the agency.

The small-town band would be on hand to play. Polly would be introduced to say a few words regarding the mission of her business. Then the honorable mayor and Mr. Tessler, the puffed-up bank president, were scheduled to talk next. The town pastor agreed to speak about the importance of establishing families and to offer a community prayer for prosperity. The church choir would follow him with a selection from the hymnal.

Once Vella had vaguely mentioned something about a surprise in store at the end of the program. She hadn't brought it up again, so Polly had forgotten about it. Then the head of the town council would do the honor of cutting the ribbon declaring Spur's mail order bride business to be officially open.

The Women's Society agreed to provide liquid refreshments and cookies in return for a sizeable donation to help support community causes. Small bags of popcorn from the local street vendor would be handed out while he played short ditties on a small accordion. His tiny, pet monkey, wearing a plaid hat with a chin strap, would dance jigs on top of the cart.

A traveling puppet wagon would provide puppet shows and hard candy for the children, and a garishly dressed man on stilts was hired to walk around so people could gawk at the oddity. There would also be a juggler.

With the marshal's permission, the agency paid a man he recommended to organize a shooting contest. Prizes would be awarded to the top three marksmen in each of two categories. The competition of skill was an effort to draw more cowboys and farmers into town. Posters were hanging all over the territory weeks in advance advertising the shooting contest and the dance to follow.

Local fiddlers would provide the dance music. The obvious dilemma of men outnumbering women would be solved diplomatically by blue bandanas tied around the men's arms who'd lead, and red bandanas tied on the arms of those who'd follow the steps. Anyone of them lucky enough to snag a girl could do so and lead all he wanted.

Some of the single men might become interested in a mail order bride. Vella kept the doors of the West to East Matrimonial Agency open all day. Citizens were encouraged to have a look and pick up flyers and catalogues printed by the newspaper office explaining how the business of ordering a bride worked.

An eye-catching, half-page invitation had been in the bi-monthly edition of the town's newspaper. After the grand opening it would be replaced by a smaller advertisement which would appear in the paper regularly.

Polly was an entrepreneur and understood networking. She also knew the value of word-of-mouth endorsements. Her respectable mail order bride business was already a hit. It hadn't gone unnoticed its service and the catalogue were already adding to the area's economy.

The day of the ribbon cutting was well attended, and the noise level of the crowd was full of laughter, clapping, and happy conversations. After the choir sang a selection from the church hymnal and just before the ribbon was cut, JD and Lilac walked onto the platform.

Polly couldn't believe her eyes, and her hand cupped her throat with a will of its own. A hush came over the crowd. It was no secret the marshal had married a mail order bride, and everyone wanted to hear what he had to say on the subject.

However, he didn't speak, but rather stood by his lovely wife with a supportive arm curled around her waist. Lilac held her head high and began to speak loudly and clearly.

"I was all alone in San Antonio. I desired both a husband and a way to leave the city behind. I'd heard good things about Polly Stearns and the East to West Matrimonial Agency located there. The day I had the courage to knock on her door and ask for help was the best decision I've ever made.

"She took me under her wing, gave me a place to live in her own house, and put me to work in her office. She had me write my own letter of introduction, but Polly didn't post it right away. Instead, she contacted JD, her nephew, and your marshal. She asked him if he'd be willing to let her find a bride for him to consider.

"He agreed. After receiving my introduction letter, he sent one back introducing himself. He wrote about your town and the territory. He wrote about the ranches and the farms. Most of all he wrote about the wonderful people here, and the dedication he had to keeping you safe.

"We continued to exchange letters, and months later I traveled here so we could be married in the church. Many of you were there to witness this. JD built a home in preparation for my arrival, and some of you helped.

"We are happily married and raising our children together in this community. Today, JD and I want to publicly express our gratitude to Aunt Polly and give our personal endorsement for the fine service she provides for others!"

JD looked directly at Polly, fingering the brim of his hat, and nodding his head to her in tribute. The crowd whooped and hollered in unison. Men whistled, and hats were thrown high in the air.

It was time to cut the yellow ribbon. When it was

severed, and the ends fell limp to the platform floor, another round of applause and cheers went up. The town band began to play again and marched all the way to the end of the street. People parted like the red sea letting them pass.

JD held his arms up signaling the crowd to be quiet. He announced the shooting competition would take place in the vacant field near the church. The first shot would be fired in half an hour! He told the contestants and those who wanted to watch to go there now.

The target shoot was a great segue from the morning's program, and by the number of spectators who walked over to watch, it was extremely popular. Men, women, and children alike were there. Families had spread patchwork quilts to sit upon with opened picnic baskets brought from home along with jugs of water.

Polly felt blessed to see so many familiar faces from Byrd Ranch. JD considered them family, and she was beginning to think of them as very close friends. In the time since she'd met them, they'd engulfed her and Martha in warmth. The idea of family was overwhelming. Moving to Spur was the best decision she ever made.

She joined Mary Ann, Belle, Qynne, the girls, and the other Byrd Ranch children on the two quilts. She was overjoyed to see Martha up close again! She'd missed her. Polly gave her ward a big hug, smoothed her hair repeatedly, and kissed her cheek with an exaggerated smack! Everyone laughed, and the attention caused the girl to smile with happiness reflecting the sunshine.

Clay and Stone were there too. They'd helped the women settle a safe distance from where the guns would be fired. Stoic as always, they touched their index fingers to their hat brims and nodded in Polly's direction. They even gifted her with discreet smiles. Her heart turned over at the sight of her two special friends, and she waved, smiled, and nodded her head back at them.

The rules for the competition were simple. Each contestant signed up to participate in either the sidearm contest or the rifle match. Only one entry per man was allowed. Shooters could only use the guns provided, not their own. They were given only three cartridges to load for each round. Twelve paper targets were lined up in a row for twelve contenders to shoot at a time.

The placement of the three shots would determine the winner of each set. In the event of a tie too close to call, two winners would advance to the second round. The second round would pit the winners against each other. The three best left standing would then face off.

First, second, and third place winners in the two categories would be declared by the judges. If the holes in the targets were absolutely too close to call, a fourth shot between the ties would be fired, and so on, until a third-place victor rose to the top. When it was all over, the prizes were handed out.

In the rifle category, a new rifle and a 1st Place Blue Ribbon went to Stone Byrd. A 2nd Place Red Ribbon was presented to a wrangler from Morten's Ranch along with a new scatter gun, and the 3rd Place Green Ribbon winner received a box of cartridges. This was awarded to the foreman of the Rocking K spread.

In the handgun category, a new revolver went to Clay Byrd with the 1st Place Blue Ribbon. The 2nd Place Red Ribbon winner received a new Derringer. It was given to Ollie Norton who was just passing through town looking for work. The 3rd Place Green Ribbon came with a box of cartridges awarded to the mayor's son.

After the excitement, Ted Rhymes approached Polly grinning like a jackass eating sticker briers. She stood and introduced him to her friends. Mr. Rhymes was polite in the exchanges but dismissive in his responses. He hooked her arm in his as a gesture of a private invitation and pulled her away from the picnic.

"Polly, you look tuckered out. Let's go sit in the shade someplace and enjoy a cool lemonade, shall we?"

"You're right, I am exhausted! I'll take you up on the offer. Thank you, Ted." she said cordially.

As they walked away, Mary Ann and Belle exchanged glances with raised eyebrows.

CHAPTER 34

---◆-◦✛◦-◆---

~*Kriss*

Kriss, the driver of the ill-fated Concord stagecoach out of Abilene, finally arrived back in town and returned to his comfortable house. He'd tactfully made his escape from his daughter's farm. She'd protested his leaving by arguing he was still recovering from the two bullet holes he'd taken to his chest in the holdup.

Kriss understood her reluctance to let him go home. He'd admit to himself he was weak as a kitten, but every day he felt his strength increasing a little more. Damn, if he hadn't gotten homesick, and dang if it didn't hurt worse than his recovery. He knew he'd rest better alone in his own place, the home he'd shared with his wife Ellen before influenza had taken her.

Their daughter, Clarice, was concerned about all the weight he'd lost. He didn't like it much either, but his appetite was coming back. He promised her to cook himself a hearty breakfast each morning, eat supper at Mabel's Boarding House, and rest every day. He'd do it too because he was bound and determined to claim his sovereignty back.

Kriss was going to be the man he'd been before he'd come so close to dying. Oh, he had no delusions he'd ever drive a stagecoach again for more reasons than one, but he'd no doubt find something he liked to do eventually.

He'd saved most of his income since Ellen passed. There was nothing extra he had the heart to buy anymore. He only purchased basic necessities. The extra sat in the bank drawing interest and growing. He had plenty enough to see him through until he could work again.

Poor Charlie! He was going to miss his good friend. They'd ridden many miles together for the Overland Stage Line and talked about everything. He planned to look in on his family often for him. Charlie had known how dangerous their jobs were, but the money for his family was too good to pass up. They both knew how vulnerable they were riding up top.

Few things surprised him anymore, but the lady passenger on the stage had caught his attention which was unusual. Then, she became the only reason he was alive today. The marshal and two different doctors had told him it was absolutely true. He didn't know what, but he owed her something.

The marshal told him about her taking over the situation and becoming the hero. She'd saved lives during the robbery and killed two of the killers by herself after everyone thought she had died. Then she refused to let Kriss die and dug the lead out of his chest herself. JD said she refused to leave his side until it was safe for him to be moved.

He'd never met a woman like her, and he wanted to see her again. She owed him rent for the space she was taking up in his head. Maybe seeing the woman would get her out of his system

The first time Kriss had laid his eyes on her, the fact she

had a pretty face angered him. It hadn't sat well with him at all. This lady had given him pause to look at her twice. He'd heaped blame on her for his unfaithfulness to his dead wife.

The real truth was Kriss had been mad ever since his wife, Ellen, died. It wasn't the lady's fault he was interested in her, but he didn't want her riding on his stage and going to his hometown. Grief had become his mantra. It was the only tune he could sing, and he was wrapped in the comfort of the self-inflicted pain.

He confronted the woman's effect on him by being a stubborn ass, bossy, and speaking rudely to her on the run from the very beginning. Kriss had put up his shields when he realized she was a danger to his misery.

Kriss had accepted his lot in life was to be alone. The last thing he wanted was to look at another woman. He'd grown accustomed to living with nothing in his life beyond memories.

It had been unbearable watching Ellen, the love of his life, being lowered into the unforgiving West Texas prairie sod. He swore he'd not love another. This land was too brutal for beautiful women, and he'd never wanted to have to bury another one.

Only a few people in town knew he'd come home, but the word would get around as fast as a wildfire. Once the news hit the grapevine, it would scatter like a horse stampede. He'd stopped at the general store first thing to get food supplies and a newspaper. The store was the hub of the community, and the aproned owner and his wife were the town criers.

Yesterday, he cooked as soon as he walked through the door of his house. He'd eaten at his daughter's before he left, but the ride home had made him hungry again. He'd stopped by the store and then tended to his horse. It was all more than he was used to doing, and his reserve of energy had been depleted. He'd gone straight to his bed after he ate.

Without the noise of grandchildren to disturb him, he'd slept straight through until daybreak. When he got up, he was hungry for another big breakfast. Then he read and rested up for tonight's outing. It would be his first supper at Mabel's table.

Entering the boarding house in the afternoon, he went straight to the kitchen to find her. The swinging door announced his entrance, before he said, "Mabel, I'd be obliged if you'd feed me tonight. I'll be a regular at supper for a while and will pay you by the week if it's alright with you."

She turned from the stove and stopped stirring whatever she was cooking.

"Why, somebody said you'd come back to town! Glory be, you have! You're a sight for sore eyes!

"Kriss, when I heard about you and Charlie getting bushwhacked, I prayed hard for you both. Later, I found out poor Charlie didn't make the cut, and then I cried and prayed for his poor little family. I've been so worried about you and praying every day since.

"Nobody in town knew if you were still among the living! Let me look at you, Kriss." She backed up an arm's length and studied her best friend's husband, shaking her head and cupping his cheeks between the palms of her hands.

"I kept thinking how upset Ellen would be if she was still with us, but today she'd be all smiles again. Land's sakes! Looks like you need to eat more than one meal a day here, I think! We've got to put some meat on your bones and get the color back in your face!"

"Just supper will do, Mabel. I feel like cooking breakfast for myself at home every morning. Then I can rest until I come here in the evening. I don't have my strength back quite yet."

"Well, of course you don't! How did you get here to the

boarding house, Kriss?"

"I walked. It's not far, and the doctor says I need to keep moving to get better. Walking is good for me."

"Ellen would be sad to see you so thin and pale, Kriss. I'll just have to fatten you up," Mabel decided. "Have a seat anywhere at the dining room table. The others will be coming in a few minutes to join you."

He was hungry enough to eat a bushel full of dried corn. Whatever Mabel was cooking sure smelled good. One of Mabel's big home-cooked meals was sounding better all the time. He was wondering what might be on the menu.

No sooner than he sat down, one of the girls who worked for Mabel came out of the kitchen to bring him a cold glass of buttermilk. She sat it by his plate.

"Mabel told me to tell you to drink all of this."

He smiled to himself. Coming here was already lifting his spirits. The feeling didn't last long though.

What the hell!

The woman he knew as Melody Potter walked into the dining room with a flouncy, feathered fascinator clipped into her upswept hair. The peculiar piece of frippery struck Kriss as a foolhardy, silly notion. The man with his possessive hand on her shoulder was nothing but a fancy-dan, and she was listening to what he was saying close to her ear!

The unexpected scene captured Kriss off guard, and he'd just taken a big gulp of Mabel's thick, rich buttermilk. The shock of seeing the scallywag hanging onto the lady caused his swallow to misfire. Some liquid escaped down his throat, but a lot of it stuck in his goozle blocking off his airhole. The rest of the sour milk was left behind to pool in his mouth. It was threatening to spew out onto the table at any moment!

Almost in one motion, he grabbed the cloth napkin, covered his mouth and part of his face, stood abruptly, and knocked his chair clean over. He fled to the kitchen hoping to get there in time to avoid making more of a spectacle than he already had. Conversation in the dining room ceased.

Maybe she hadn't recognized him. He'd dropped over twenty pounds, shaved away his whiskers, and held the cloth to his face. The stagecoach driver didn't know why he even cared, but this female had gotten under his skin the moment he'd seen her in Abilene. He didn't want her to see him like this.

Just as he remembered, she was pretty as a picture. He also remembered her saucy mouth. She had not been hesitant to stand right up to him. She handed out as good as she got. It was plenty to recommend a woman to a man like him. Kriss had found her spunk irresistible. As if all this wasn't tempting enough, she'd single-handedly saved his bacon out on the trail after those mad dogs shot him!

When he got to the kitchen, he made a beeline for the back door to spit and cough up what he could to clear his airway. Once he'd gotten rid of most of it, his throat was left raw and burning from one ear to the other it seemed. What a relief it was to get his fill of air again!

"What on earth, Kriss? What happened to you? Are you alright?" A concerned Mabel rushed behind her friend out onto the porch and pounded him on his back.

After a minute of continually clearing his throat, he'd recovered enough to grate out a few gravelly words.

"Mable, I, I guess I, uggg, wasn't as ready for a public outing as I thought, ugggmmm."

"Oh, my! Come and sit down in the kitchen, Kriss. I'll get you some water to drink, while I wrap your supper up. You take it home with you. For the rest of the week, I'll send one of the girls over to your place with a plate. You can try coming back again after you get to feeling better."

CHAPTER 35

A FANCY-DAN

The next afternoon, Kriss was nodding off in his soft, upholstered chair. He was worn out as usual. A knock at the door roused him. He assumed it was one of the girls from the boardinghouse bringing supper.

He called out, "Come in, the door is unlocked."

When Melody Potter sashayed into his house, the sight of her all pink, clean, and fresh got his goat. The flowery smell wafting around her was almost intoxicating. Dad-burn-it, she'd caught him off guard again!

Is this damn woman everywhere?

"What in tarnation are you doin' here, Ms. Potter?"

"First off, my name really isn't Melody or Potter. It's Polly Stearns. I just traveled to Spur under an alias. It seemed safer, I thought, but it didn't turn out to be, did it?"

He ignored her observation. "Stearns, as in Marshal JD Stearns?"

"Yes, I'm his aunt."

"Really?

"You saved my life, Ms. Stearns. I'da died if it hadn't been for your doctorin'. I don't know how you knew what to do!"

"Not the only bullets I'd ever fished out of a man. Lucky for you! Wasn't it?"

And there's the sass! Music to my ears!

"After the gagging spell you had at the boarding house yesterday, I came to deliver your supper from Mabel. I wanted to see for myself how you're doing, Kriss."

"Oh, you witnessed me get sick, did you?

"You needn't have bothered. Buttermilk just went down the wrong way. Could've happened to anybody."

"Really? From where I'm standing right now, you look terrible! You look like I could reach out and knock you clean over."

"Mmmmm! Try it!

"Ms. Stearns, you have a wicked bedside manner, but why am I not surprised? You are the most plain-spoken female I ever met!

"Do me a favor and leave the food in the kitchen and don't let the door hit you on the way out. If it's all the same to you, I'll eat by myself in peace."

"And you think you're not the most overbearing man I've ever met? Don't think I can be brushed off so easily, you old sourpuss. I'll leave when I get good and ready to go, and you're too frail and weak to do anything about it!

"Like it or not, I'm invested in your health. I didn't dig those hunks of lead from your chest just to watch you die from a drink of buttermilk! I came to see for myself how you're healing."

"Well, don't expect me to take my shirt off for you!"

"Mmmph! Don't flatter yourself, I've already seen your physique once and don't want to look at it again."

She took the covered basket and sat it on the kitchen table. When she returned, she made herself right at home, next to him in the rocking chair. The sight of her in Ellen's chair made him feel raw and crawly inside.

"Kriss, Let's don't be mean to each other. I'm so sorry you were shot. I'm glad I was there and knew how to help. I'm so happy you're alive. The first time we met, I thought you were the bossiest, rudest man I'd ever heard, but I don't think it's true.

"I had a stubborn attitude, and I was ready to spar after the uncomfortable trip I'd already had. I took your orders personally and boiled over. But after everything went to hell in a handbasket, I realized you were just trying to get your passengers safely from one place to another. You had a difficult job to do. The weight of the responsibility you carried didn't dawn on me until after the ambush. I'm grateful you and Charlie did what you could to save us. It was a no-win situation."

"Yeah, well, don't worry about my feelings! I'm not some flashy, fancy-dan like the fake admirer hooked onto you at Mabel's yesterday. My feelings don't get hurt easily."

"The fake admirer? You mean, are you talking about Ted Rhymes? He and I are just acquaintances. He's not a bad sort." She further dismissed his insinuations with a dismissive wave.

"Whether he's my admirer or not is none of your business, Mr. Wagon Master. We're not on the stage now!"

"You may be as skinny as a bean pole and pale as a skeleton, but you're still as ill-tempered as ever! I don't feel charitable toward you anymore. My coming here today was a mistake I won't be making again. I should have known a leopard doesn't change his spots!"

"Polly Stearns," he warned, pointing his finger at her. "If I was you, I'd watch my step around Mr. Fancy Pants. I've seen dudes a plenty like him riding the circuits to the next town looking for another easy mark. Swindlers particularly prey on ripe, old, well-to-do widder ladies."

"I'm not a widow. I've never found a man I thought was

good enough to marry."

"Now why am I not surprised you never found a man who'd have you? Just the same, I'm warning you right now to be careful. Keep your eye on your pocketbook."

Polly got up so fast, it set Ellen's chair rocking. She left exasperated without saying goodbye. The door slammed shut behind her while Ellen's memorial rocking chair was still in motion.

Kriss was hard put to say why it mattered a twit to him, one way or another, if Polly Stearns was upset, or if the fickle woman was letting a swindler court her. But for some reason, it rankled him an awful lot. No good could come from a man sniffing around her like Ted Rhymes or whoever he was.

Tomorrow, I'll have a talk with her nephew.

He gloomily ate his supper in the kitchen and went to bed disgruntled. Being in his own house, eating good food, and getting plenty of rest were the only things he needed. He didn't need Polly Stearns or anyone else looking after him!

After a breakfast of sliced ham, red rust gravy, three eggs over easy, and two thick slices of buttered toast with two cups of coffee, he walked to the marshal's office. He found JD behind his desk doing paperwork.

The marshal stood up and offered his hand to him.

"Kriss, you old son of a gun, I heard you were back in town and doing much better than the last time I saw you laid out on the prairie! I've been in and out on business for a few days or I would have already been over to see you.

"Before I left out of town this last time, I stopped by to check on Charlie's family. His wife and kids are taking what happened hard, of course, but they're getting' by. He was a good man, Charlie was. The church and town are rallying around to help them. For the time being, they're gonna try and stay in Spur."

"I'm glad to hear it, Marshal. Thanks for telling me. I need to get over there."

"Kriss, did you just stop by to jaw, or is something on your mind?"

"I guess something is troubling me though I've been told it's none of my business."

JD smiled. "Sit down, and I'll pour us some coffee. I've got time to talk."

Once they were both settled with their cups, JD laughed, "Now, tell me what's none of your business."

Kriss chuckled, "Well, JD it's about your Aunt."

"Polly, you mean?" JD couldn't believe it.

"JD, how many aunts do you have living in this town? I know I've been gone awhile and maybe I lost count."

"Funny, Kriss, real funny! I just got the one, and I figure you know it," the marshal grinned. "Probably a good thing too. She's a handful!

"What about Aunt Polly?"

"She stopped by to see how I'm getting' along since she saved my life and all."

"For certain, she did pull your hide from the fire, Kriss. It's a good thing she was on your stage."

"Oh, yeah, I'm not forgetting. In fact, I owe her big time!

"Anyhow, since I got back to Spur, I'm taking my suppers at Mabel's Boarding House. The first night I was there, Polly walked in on the arm of a city slicker."

"I saw her with him I think, right after the shooting contest over by the church house. He was wearing a city suit and a derby hat, stuck out like a sore thumb!"

"Yeah, he's the one. They're both boarding at Mabel's, and eating together, and I don't know what all. They're chummy, I'd say. The point is I don't like it, JD. I've seen a lot of dudes like him riding the stages looking for an unsuspecting female to charm out of a buck.

"It's not right for him to be sniffing around your Aunt Polly and thought you should know."

"Do you have a name?"

"Ted, something or other, Ted, let me think, Ted Rhymes."

"If you're thinking I need to look into this man, your opinion's good enough for me, Kriss. I don't want Aunt Polly to get in trouble and hurt by a man any more than she already has been. She's been dealt one real bad hand already. Life has been too hard on her.

"I'll talk to him and get a feel for what he's doing here. If I think it's needed, I'll get his name out on the wire and do a little fishing, myself.

"I'm glad I came to see you then, JD. I feel better you're gonna look into this. Your Aunt Polly needs someone looking out for her."

"Well, Kriss, it sounds to me like you are! Are you interested in Aunt Polly?"

"Nothing like you're thinking, JD. I just think she's a special woman. I don't want a man taking advantage of her."

"I see. Oh, an' Kriss, keep on keeping an eye on her for me. I can't be everywhere at once. I'll let you know what I find out after I talk to this Ted Bowling." The two men shook hands.

After Kriss was gone, JD shook his head and grinned.

Polly and Kriss, wouldn't that be something! I didn't see it coming!

CHAPTER 36

——◆◈◆——

THE MAN WHO LOVED A GHOST

~Polly

The visit to Kriss's house yesterday had blown up, but he wasn't the only one at fault. This man had a way of making Polly spit sand. He had an opinionated nature and, no doubt, baited her. But she didn't know how to keep her mouth shut and sharp words tumbled out before she could shut it.

Then around they'd go with her baiting him! The two could sure get each other's hackles up. Polly thought she should wipe the dust off her boots and not look back, but she couldn't. She was a glutton for punishment. Lord, help her, he was the only man she wanted.

She only found out the day before yesterday he'd survived the shooting. Polly was so relieved to see him at the boarding house, and then she was equally frightened when he'd suddenly gotten strangled.

There had been a great chance he wouldn't make it even

after she'd removed the bullets. His daughter and son-in-law took Kriss to their farm once the doctor had done all he could for him. It had been the right plan to let his family nurse him, but she'd heard nothing after he left.

There were so many things she admired about Kriss. She'd liked his full head of dark wavy, hair streaked with licks of silver. How she wanted to run her hands through it. He was tall, muscular, and strong. His face was striking with symmetrical features and thick, kissable lips. She'd never thought about kissing a man's lips before!

It hurt her to see him so thin and weak now, but he'd get his bulk and power back. A man like Kriss who was too tough to die and prevailing enough to handle teams of spirited horses pulling heavy loads would rise like the phoenix. He was a unique bird.

Polly respected his authoritative nature and admired a man who could stand up to her. A near death experience hadn't dampened Kriss's spirit one little bit!

Polly admitted she was seven different kinds of a fool to think Kriss could ever want her for his woman. Polly derided herself a hundred times over for falling in love with the rough-edged, bossy cowboy who wore scuffed boots and a dusty black Stetson. He actually made them look good.

I love a man who still loves a ghost. I'm pathetic.

Oh, she knew about Ellen. She'd asked Mabel about Kriss and actually learned more about Ellen. Their stories couldn't be told separately. The two of them loved each other with absolute devotion. Their relationship was of the kind written in romance novels.

They'd known each other all their lives and were destined to be married. No one ever thought otherwise. Ellen was a lady in every sense of the word. She was beautiful, kind, thoughtful, and a homemaker. He built her a house, and she made it a home. They had one daughter, Clarice. The pregnancy and birth were hard and broke her health.

She never completely recovered, and they could never risk having another child. She was susceptible to colds, fevers, and any illness passable from one human being to another. She got along for several years and even saw Clarice married and settled.

The very next winter an influenza epidemic hit. Several in the area died, and Ellen was one of them. Kriss was devastated and grieved so hard he has never completely let Ellen rest in peace.

He started driving for the Overland Stage Company because it was a hard, reckless, and dangerous job. It kept Kriss away from Ellen's house for long periods of time after her death. Being the kind of man he is, he took the driver's job very seriously. Caring for the safety of his passengers gave him a purpose to go on living.

It had been over a week since the quarrel with Kriss. His opinion of Ted Rhymes made her see he was right. Ted was all hat and no cattle. He was indeed fake and polished and his egotism had worn too thin on her nerves.

She tried weening him off gently, but he wouldn't take the hint. She had decided it was time to be blunt and break ties with him without mincing words.

Before she got around to running him off, JD showed up at Mabel's and asked to speak outside with Ted Rhymes. The next morning, the man was gone without a word. He'd cleaned his room out lock, stock, and barrel. She didn't know what business the marshal had with Ted, but his disappearance correlated with his visit. Ted Rhymes being gone suited her nicely.

She was pleased when Kriss returned to the boarding house to eat his supper. She looked at him differently since Mabel had filled her in about his wife's tragic death. She'd listen to him more carefully now and not be so quick to rile him.

Even though he could make a saint swear, Kriss needed a softer hand. Polly decided to try and be gentler with him. It wasn't a crime he'd been so in love with his wife, he'd denied his own happiness.

At supper they both acted as if their unpleasant conversation had never taken place. It was a good place to start for both of them. He looked healthier with a few pounds added, and he was stronger. Kriss even made small-talk and laughed with guests around the table. It was pleasant to see him interact sociably.

After dessert, he bowled her over by asking if she'd care to sit with him on the porch swing. For once, she didn't retort with a pithy comeback. She grabbed her shawl while he waited at the bottom of the stairs for her. She tried not to hurry, but she felt like a girl. She didn't know what to expect next.

At first, they just sat quietly, pushing the heavy swing back and forth with their feet for a while. It was enough, but Kriss finally sighed and then started talking.

"Polly, I've been remiss in thanking you properly for not letting me die on the prairie. For the past couple of years, I haven't cared if I lived or died."

Polly hadn't expected a thank you for the part she'd played in saving his life. She'd dug those slugs out because she knew how to do it, and she saw too good a man to give up on without a fight. She sensed there was more he wanted to say, so she waited for him to continue.

"I really thought I didn't care if I lived or died, but I've found out differently. I'm not ready to check it out yet. You gave me a second chance at life. You gave me the chance to realize I want to live again, and I'm not going to waste it being alone.

"I knew something was changing inside of me the first time I saw you in Abilene.

"You were so pretty and sure of yourself, and I was afraid for you. I didn't think you were ready for this rugged prairie. It's a hard place for beautiful, gentle women to make it." He chuckled.

"I had no idea what a tough lady you are, Polly Stearns, but you've taught me a thing or two. Yes, you have, Darlin'."

"I'm sorry for giving you a hard time. I've been upset with myself because you were the first woman, I'd allowed myself to see, I mean really look at since my wife passed.

"Polly, I have a daughter, so you already knew at some point I was married. My wife died too young. Her name was Ellen, and I loved her more than breathing, I thought.

"I still love her and always will, but after meeting you and coming so close to death, I'm not ready to leave this earth, Polly. I've been wallowing in grief like it's a place to stay. I'm ready to move on and put the past to rest.

"I'm tired of living with a ghost."

"I'd like to start with you and me being friends. Would you want to try, Polly?"

"Kriss, I'd be proud to be your friend."

"Well, friend, how would you like to take your horse out tomorrow, go for a ride, and have a picnic."

"Hell, yeah! I'll use Mabel's kitchen and pack a basket for us."

"I'll be around after breakfast. JD told me where your mare is stabled behind your business. I'll saddle him for you and bring him over.

"You talked to JD?"

"Of course I did. I can't court another man's mama without asking him first, can I?"

"He told you about me."

"Yes, he's very proud of you, Polly, and wants you to find joy and happiness. He gave us his blessing."

"Tomorrow, Polly, I want you to take me to this house Deet's is building for you."

"You know about the house? You know Deets?

"Honey, I know everything about you. How would I take care of you if I don't?"

Kriss put his lips on Polly's mouth and moved his across hers like he'd never stop. It took her breath away, and she felt things she'd never felt. She'd never experienced a genuine kiss before, and she melted into this man.

True to Polly's nature, she gave back as good as she got!

ABOUT THE AUTHOR

Jana Dahmen just finished writing The Byrd Ranch Series and can hardly wait to share the trilogy with her readers. The three titles of the historical fiction series in order are *Broken Pieces, Qynne's Canyon,* and *The Byrd Ranch Legacy.* Each of the three volumes can be enjoyed as a standalone, but avid readers will want to know the panorama of the whole story.

How many Byrds does it take to feather a nest? The tight knit brood of the Byrd family with the added bonus of friends much closer than acquaintances can best be illustrated by the old saying, "Birds of a Feather Flock Together."

The Byrd Ranch Trilogy traces family and friends back to the settling of the West Texas tall grass prairie land in the 1800's. The intertwined lives, heritages, and situations read like a patchwork quilt of adventures in the Old West.

Sharon Kizziah-Holmes at Paperback Press is her friend, mentor, and an author in her own right. Jana couldn't have finished this series without Sharon's encouragement and the hard work of Paperback Press!

All of Jana's books to date can be purchased on Amazon or by contacting her at jdahmen@att.net

She's presently writing The Cameo Trail.

www.ingramcontent.com/pod-product-compliance
Lightning Source LLC
Chambersburg PA
CBHW051432170626
46809CB00006B/2431